TOO MUCH

R AND R

BOOK TWO

Jacob Gunter

ISBN# **9798294747732** (Paperback)

Copyright 2024 Jacob Gunter
All Rights Reserved

Illustrations and cover design by Fritz Gunter from Iamfritz.com

All rights reserved. No part of this publication may be reproduced, distributed, or transmitted in any form or by any means, including photocopying, recording, or other electronic or mechanical methods without prior written permission of the publisher.

Contents

1. Remembrance 1
2. The Fallen 9
3. Command Center 19
4. Recon byMud 23
5. Target Practice 36
6. What Went Wrong? 49
7. Enjoy The Little Things 57
8. It Begins 61
9. Not His Fault 69
10. I'm in Charge 75
11. Larger World 86
12. Not Again 102
13. Lucious 108
14. What Comes Next...................................... 117
15. Meeting of Grave Importance..................... 124
16. We're With You 139
17. Calm Day 147
18. Negotiations 153
19. Jace's Deal 167
20. The Fight 169
21. No More 178
22. Him Again 182
23. Give Peace a Chance 191
24. Bad Idea 196
25. Bad To Worse 205
26. Heart To Heart 219
27. The Plan 226
28. Radio 232
29. They Know 238
30. Once More 249
31. Late Night Chat 254
32. Ambush 260
33. This is Bad 271
34. Shadow.. 276

Remembrance

Rose and Fi stand together on the balcony overlooking the courtyard of their citadel.

"Now that the fighting has stopped, we should take some time to remember everyone we lost along the way," Rose says.

"Keep their memories going," Fi says in agreement.

"Yes. We wouldn't be here if not for the actions of others. We can't let them be forgotten," Rose says.

"I agree. We should set up a memorial for them," Fi suggests.

"That's a great idea.

"James, who hid my brother and I when our city was destroyed. Jon, who gave us shelter at the capital until the machines destroyed it," Rose says.

"Jon definitely helped a lot of people. Not perfect, but he tried," Fi adds.

"Even Summer."

"Even Summer?" Fi asks surprised.

"Even Summer, she led us out of the capital to here. She helped us find my parents," Rose says softly.

"That is true. She was a great friend. Just wish things ended differently," Fi says, saddened.

"Yeah. Especially with my brother."

"Rand was a family man. He put his family before everything, even himself," Fi says.

"He always put me first. He killed our parents for me when they were working for Aida," Rose says, even sadder.

"He had good intentions."

Rose turns to Fi. "I have to keep his memory alive. I won't let him be forgotten."

"It won't be easy for anyone to forget Rand. He left a mark on everyone he met. Whether good or bad," Fi says.

"We just need to make sure the good goes on," Rose says.

"Alright, enough of this, I'm too tired to be sad. What are your plans for now?" Fi asks, leaning on the railing.

"Why are you asking me? We lead together," Rose says, joining in leaning beside Fi.

"I'm more of an adviser than a leader," Fi says. "You've got heart, you're definitely the better choice for a leader than me."

"You really think so? I don't know how to lead. I can't be responsible for the lives of others," Rose starts.

"Hey, don't doubt yourself. Yes, losing people is tough, especially when they rely on you. You can't focus on that, you have to focus on the bigger picture. What the fight is for," Fi says, turning to face her again.

"I just don't know if I can lead," Rose says.

"Why not?" Fi asks.

"I'm young, everyone here has more experience than me," she says.

"But not everyone here could hold Rand back like you."

"I'm just a little girl. I don't think anyone would actually follow if I was the leader," she finally says.

"So that's what this is about," Fi says, looking over the balcony. "What do you think is going through their minds when they see you lead?"

"I don't know," Rose says.

"I can assure you, it's not about your age or being a girl. These guys know what you did. What you sacrificed. They respect that. That's what leadership is about," Fi looks over making eye contact with Rose, "Respect."

"Thanks Fi. Still, I would like you by my side through all of this."

"What makes you think I'd ever leave?" Fi asks.

"I mean leading. We lead together," Rose says.

"I guess Rand would want me keeping you out of trouble, so I accept," Fi says.

"Thanks. I need to think," Rose says, smiling.

"You're welcome, I need to sleep," Fi says.

"I would say goodnight, but it's mid day," Rose says, looking up.

"I would say you look good, but you're still wearing clothes with your own blood stains," Fi jokes.

"I did say to let me change, this is your fault," Rose teases back.

"That white jacket does look good though," Fi says, back pedaling away. They both smile as Fi disappears around the corner.

"I have to keep my family's name going," Rose says to herself as Fi leaves. *We need to hold a memorial for everyone we lost*, she thinks to herself. She goes to the stairs inside to meet with the new recruits in the courtyard.

"Greetings!" Rose says, walking in front of the recruits. "I am Rose, I'm sure you all already met Fi. We run this place together."

"You look very young," one says, surprised.

"Leadership doesn't reflect age," Rose says. "Fi and I have done great things together. And now you will do great things with us," she says smiling.

"What kind of great things?" he asks.

"Our main goal is to rebuild society. We have already sent out scouts all over, joining everyone together. This task may seem hard or out of reach, but together it will be easy," Rose says, trying to motivate them.

"How is rebuilding society easy?"

"With one person solving a problem, they need to come up with one hundred percent of the solution. With one hundred people involved, you only need each person to come up with one percent of the solution. The more people we have, the easier this will be," Rose says.

"And if none of those one hundred people get along? You can't expect everyone to bend the knee."

"You're not slaves," Rose says confused. "No one needs to bend the knee. We're rebuilding civilization together."

"And for those that don't want to be a part of your civilization?"

"No one is forced. Everyone has their freedom still," Rose says.

"What's to entice everyone to live under your rules?" He asks.

"Prosperity. Everyone that brings something to the table gets to sit at it," she says.

"So everyone that doesn't work for you starves?" He asks.

Rose glares at him, "You just can't get past me being a leader."

"I can't get past how a child is leading an army and as you said, rebuilding civilization," he says, towering over her.

"You don't know me yet, so I'll just leave you with this, don't underestimate my resolve. Fi can fill you in if you need any info," she says, walking away from him. "For now, just join the others in unarmed drills. Fi will get you guys into shape later."

Rose walks over to the gate, "Eyo," she says.

"Um, what?" The gatekeeper asks.

"Eyo," Rose repeats.

"Um, eyo?" He says back confused.

"I'm just mixing things up a bit," Rose says.

"Is that like a code word or something? Are we doing code words now?" He asks.

"No, it just means hello," she says.

"Oh, well why didn't you just say hello?" He asks.

"Mixing things up," Rose says smiling.

"But why?" He asks, confused.

"Trying to become my own person. Mixing things up in a fun, cheery way that makes people smile. People will definitely remember my parents and my brother for the bad things they did, I just want people to remember me for good things. Hopefully bring back some of that respect to my family that was lost."

"Alright, I like that. Everyone here already respects you, you don't need to worry about that," he says.

Rose shrugs and asks, "What's your name? Everyone calls you gatekeeper and I feel a little bad for not addressing you by your name."

"Oh don't worry about it, I am the gatekeeper, the keeper of the gate, it's what I do," he says with a laugh.

"I mean it. I want to show you guys respect too, what's your name?" She asks again.

"Filip," he says with a smile.

"Thank you for an exemplary job, Filip: the Keeper of the Gate," Rose says.

"Haha, thank you for your leadership and respect," Filip says.

"I do my best," she says with a smile.

Rose sees some of her people running drills and teaching the new recruits about the weapons there so she joins in. She knows the basics from her father, she knows as much about guns and gun safety as Rand did just without the practice. Rose joins in the training until Fi wakes up.

"Hey guys, what did I miss?" Fi asks, meeting up with Rose.

"Got enough beauty sleep? It's only been half a day," Rose says sarcastically.

"Tell you what, if you carry my unconscious body home after a fight I'll let you sleep as long as you want," Fi says.

"I already sleep as long as I want," Rose says back.

"So what's the problem with me sleeping?" Fi asks.

"Nothing. Just messing with you," Rose says.

"Oh haha," Fi says, sarcastically.

"Anyway, I would like to retrieve our fallen from the last fight to set up a memorial," Rose says.

"I think that's a great idea," Fi says.

"I would like to go now, so hit the guard shack to gear up," Rose says.

"Who are we taking?" Fi asks, heading towards the guard shack. "Have you thought of that yet?"

"What were the numbers? Like eight are rifle trained?" Rose asks.

"We have eight left of our assault force. A few set as defense, and I don't trust these new guys with guns yet," Fi says.

"Okay, so we can just take the eight and some of the new recruits to help with the bodies," Rose suggests.

"Alright, we should bring the tables we built to carry the machine parts for the bodies," Fi suggests.

"Good idea. Let's get everyone together," Rose says, turning her attention to the soldiers running drills. "Alright, listen up," Rose says too quietly for anyone to hear. She tries again, "listen up," still no response.

"Attention everyone," Fi shouts loudly. "Rose has some important things to say, listen up."

The entire courtyard goes silent as everyone faces towards Fi.

"Thanks Fi," she says smiling. "We're going to retrieve our fallen and set up a memorial for them here. The eight of you that came back with us last time arm up. As well as eight of the new recruits chosen by Fi," she says loudly.

"Chosen by me?" Fi says confused.

"Find eight that you trust with weapons and let's go," Rose says. "I'll be at the gate," she says walking away.

"Eyo, Filip," Rose says as she gets to the gate.

"Eyo, my lady," Filip replies. "What's on the agenda for today?"

"We're bringing home our fallen. Set them to rest," Rose says.

"That's good to hear. Thank you," he says.

"All set," Fi says, coming up from behind startling her.

"Ah, okay. So we're all set?" Rose asks.

"Yup. Let's go," Fi says.

"Filip, if you be so kind," Rose says, gesturing to the gate.

"You got it, my lady," Filip says, opening the gate.

As they all exit the gate Rose remembers, "Communication. Do we have any radiomen?"

"Yeah, Jeremy here is our radioman," Fi says, gesturing to the man.

"Ma'am," he starts, "I got us covered loud and clear."

"Oh good. Okay, well let's proceed to the machines headquarters," Rose says, leading the charge with Fi.

The Fallen

After hours of walking, they find the base once again. Just as destroyed as they remember it.

Fi shivers as they enter, seeing the interior just bringing back bad memories. "I hate this place," Fi says.

Rose is now picking up on the feeling too. "I wasn't actually prepared for this. Not emotionally," she says, remembering coming here with her brother.

"Me neither. But it's good that we're doing this," Fi says.

"That I do agree with," Rose says. "This place is empty, should we split half upstairs half downstairs?"

"I really hate the idea of splitting up," Fi says. "But I do understand. This place is abandoned," Fi looks back to Rose for her final verdict.

"Maybe, two with us and the rest together. We only brought two with us when we assaulted this place, only three bodies to bring back including my-," Rose takes a deep breath. "Including my brother."

"I'll take care of him for you," Fi says in a comforting tone.

"Okay," Rose says, straightening her composure, "So we only need two with us."

"I don't quite trust your skills that much yet," Fi says.

"I've been practicing a lot, I'm pretty good," Rose says.

"Oh, I would love to see some of that practice when we get back. But for now, let's take at least four with us. We're bringing back Summer too," Fi says.

"Okay, four with us, that leaves fourteen clearing the first floor, okay," Rose says.

Fi and Rose move slowly taking point, they clear each room with their soldiers. They get to the room where Rand executed a dozen unarmed technicians.

"Wait, where are the bodies?" Rose asks.

"Wait, yeah. I was so focused looking for our men I didn't even notice there aren't any bodies at all," Fi says.

"You guys see any bodies?" Rose asks the four soldiers accompanying them.

"No sir," they say.

"I don't understand, if their bodies are gone," Rose interrupts her own thought, "Brother!" She runs out to the next room to see the puddle of blood and her old jacket, but no Rand. Even the dagger is gone.

"You don't think he got up and walked away," Fi says with a pause.

"He, he was dead," Rose says, noticing bloody boot prints. "Fi, tell me those are your boot prints," she says pointing to them.

"No, those are wider than mine. Could be our other troops, we did leave in a hurry," Fi says.

Rose looks to the feet of the two soldiers with them, looking at their boots.

"Let's check for Summer, hopefully she stayed put," Fi says, leading the others into the next room.

Same as before, blood stains where they died, but no bodies with more bloody boot prints.

"That's impossible," Fi says, "I shot her in the head."

"Somethings not right," Rose says. "I want every room searched. Every closet empty. I don't want someone to have my brother's body. He needs to be buried with our parents."

"We'll find them," Fi says, putting a hand on her shoulder. "Let's follow the blood."

The blood wasn't fresh when they were moved so the boot prints don't go too far from each body.

"Everyone spread out," Rose says.

"I don't think that's a wise idea," Fi says. "We're still in unknown territory."

"We haven't seen anyone here, dead or alive," Rose says back.

"Doesn't mean we won't," Fi says back.

"I need everything checked. If we split up it'll be faster," Rose says, arguing.

"I don't want to argue with you, two man teams," Fi compromises.

"Fine, two man teams," Rose agrees.

"Rose I'll stay with you," Fi says, turning to the others with them. "We got this side up here, you get the other side of this floor."

"You got it," the soldiers say, heading out of the room.

"Nothing? How? Not even any blood smears. As if they just stood up and walked away," Rose says frustratedly, regrouping with her troops.

"I don't get it. We should've seen something. It's almost as if the attack here never happened," Fi says.

"Let's search around the outside, maybe we can find something out there that can give us a clue as to where they went," Rose says.

They get back to the front doors to see it pouring rain.

"Of course. Nothing is going our way today," Rose says.

"If there are any tracks that rain would wash them away, we need to hurry," Fi says.

"Everyone split up," Rose says, "try to stay in view of each other and call out if you see anything."

"Alright, let's move," Fi says, rushing out and going around the corner.

Rose carefully analyzes the front of the fortress, getting close from the rain's bad visibility. She follows the wall around the back. She sees a cloaked figure just barely visible in the open field. Thinking it's Fi, she approaches quickly. That's when she notices parts of the field are more muddy than others. She crouches down to investigate it.

The cloaked man approaches, taking an odd mix of short strides and long strides, making a weird shambling approach. More weird abnormal movements and wobbling. Rose puts her hand on her gun and stands up cautiously.

"Almost like graves," the figure says, jumping over a mound of mud.

Rose is relieved to see it is just Fi. "What did you say?" She asks, watching him awkwardly step over another mud mound to get next to her.

"These mud pits, they're almost like graves. The length, the distance apart. I think these are our people," Fi says.

"How many did we lose?" Rose asks, confused.

"Well not all of our people, we didn't see any bodies inside. Maybe someone came by and buried them too," Fi says.

"But they're our people. That doesn't make sense for someone else to bury our dead," Rose says.

"Yeah, nothing about this makes any sense," Fi says.

"I. I don't want my brother buried out here. He needs to be home," Rose says.

"Rose, it wouldn't be right digging up every body until we found your brother. I know you want him close, but he's at rest now. Let's leave him to rest," Fi says, putting his arm over her shoulder.

"I need to confirm he's here first," Rose says, holding onto his hand.

"I understand. How do you want to do that?" Fi asks.

"I don't know, maybe a sign or something. Maybe they left my jacket over him on his grave or something," Rose says. "Any kind of headstone."

"Alright, we can walk through this together," Fi says, removing his hand from her shoulder, but still holding onto her hand.

"Thank you. I'm sure this is just as emotional for you as it is for me," Rose says, holding onto his hand.

"It is. I may not have known these soldiers well, but we still lost them. It's always hard losing people. Especially a good friend," Fi says.

The two walk through the field, walking between every grave, looking closely at all of them. Nothing remarkable stands out. They head back towards the building when Fi notices something standing up at the front of the makeshift graveyard.

"That might help," Fi says, pointing in a manner that Rose can't see.

"What?" Rose asks, trying in vain to see where he's pointing.

"Let's look at that," Fi says, picking up the pace with Rose in tow.

They reach the strange object sticking out of the ground to see writing on it. "The courageous Rand and his people lay here. Fought well till the end," it reads.

Fi reads it or loud, "Woah, now that I wasn't expecting."

Rose looks confused, "Did one of our people do this?" Rose asks.

"I have no idea," Fi says.

"Was everyone accounted for when I was out?" Rose asks.

"Again, I have no idea. Everyone was too beaten up to really do anything but rest. But for someone to have his name and know what we were doing here, it had to be one of us," Fi says.

Rose says what they were both thinking, "but no one liked my brother that much aside from us. He treated his troops horribly, they wouldn't put something up like this."

"Yeah. Nothing adds up," Fi repeats.

Just then a soldier comes around the corner out of breath and panicking, "Finally, I found you," he says of breath. He turns around and shouts, "They're over here!" Then closes the distance to get right up to Fi and Rose panting out of breath.

"What is it? Are we in danger?" Fi asks.

"Yes," the soldier says in-between heavy breaths.

"What is it?" Fi says, urgently, drawing his rifle.

Rose grabs her rifle from her sling, "Where is it?" She asks.

"Tracks," he says.

"Tracks?" Fi asks, confused.

"Big tracks," the soldier says, still panting.

"Spit it out," Fi says. "If we're in danger I need to know everything now."

"More tracks, leading to the building and away," he says.

"Like machines came here after we destroyed the targeting computer?" Fi asks.

Rose's eyes widen, "So there are still big machines out there, and we are armed with little rifles."

"We need to regroup everyone back at base, we need to check the map," Fi says.

"Right away," the soldier says, finally catching his breath. "Everyone is at the front of the building."

"Lead the way," Fi says, running along close behind.

When they reach the main force, one asks, "Fi, did you find anything?"

Fi completely ignores him and calls out, "Where's Jeremy? I need the radio."

"Right here, boss," Jeremy says. "What do you need to say?" He says, taking the radio off his back.

"Tell Home Base the machines are still operational and to be on guard with the heavy weapons on the gate," Fi says.

"Roger that," Jeremy says, fiddling with the radio, "Home Base, this is Jeremy, how copy?"

A moment of silence until, "Jeremy this is home base, send traffic over," comes over the radio.

"Home base, be advised the machines are still running around, repeat; machines are still at large, over."

"Jeremy, how can this be? Didn't we take out the targeting controls? Over."

"Affirm on that, but we found tracks here that appear to be more recent than our assault. Fi wants more personnel on the defenses, we haven't found any contact but we need to be ready. Fi also says to check out the map that tracks the machines, over."

"Copy that, I'll send more troops to the walls and on the perimeter defenses at once, I don't see anything out of the ordinary on the map. Stand by for a closer look, over."

"What does any of that mean?" Rose says confused.

"Right, you're probably the only one here that doesn't have military experience," Fi says.

"Wait, you were in the military? You're a little young for that, aren't you?" Rose asks, adding to her confusion.

"I wasn't old enough to be in the field, but I was old enough to go through the training," Fi says.

"Well that explains your shooting, so what does any of that mean?" Rose asks again.

"You're going to need to specify," Fi says. "What did you understand from it?"

"Not anything really," Rose says, thinking for a moment. "I got the machines running around, the part about assaulting the targeting center, and reinforcing our walls."

"So you got all of it," Fi says.

"I guess, but the words for everything, I didn't get that stuff," Rose says.

"Well we need to get back to Home Base now, we can talk about it on the way," Fi says, then turning to the rest of the troops, "Let's move out. Back to Home Base."

"Jeremy to Home Base, we're on our way back, over."

"Jeremy, we read you. Be advised, there is subtle activity on the board. I advise you to double time it and get here fast, over."

"Copy all, over," Jeremy says, looking back at Fi.

"Okay, we need to get back to Home Base asap. Let's move," Fi says, leading the way.

Command Center

After a long exhausting run, they make it back to their home base.

"Filip, open the gate," Rose calls out.

"Who's Filip?" Fi asks.

"The gatekeeper," Rose says, as the gate opens. "Thanks Filip."

"Everyone that was with us, rest. We need everyone ready for a fight at any moment," Fi says to the men. "You're with me," he says to Rose.

"To the control room?" Rose asks.

"Yes," Fi says, running off with Rose next to him.

The map in the control room is a big table with a computer screen along the surface with an electronic map that tracks the machines.

Fi and Rose run over to the map. "That's a lot of movement," Fi says surprised.

"I don't understand, how are they operating without their targeting computer?" Rose asks.

"Or why haven't they attacked us?" Fi asks.

"None of this makes sense. Should we send an assault force or scouts to see what's up?" Rose asks.

"These could just be transponders that people removed from the machines," Fi says.

"Transponder? What's that?" Rose asks.

"Transponder, the tracking part," Fi says. "Used in a way to keep track of all your people. Each squad leader has one so you can track their movements better."

"That would mean we aren't the only ones able to track them," Rose says.

Fi looks panicked, "they might have a secondary targeting facility. Maybe they realized we are a threat and have been gathering all their machines to attack us."

"I'll analyze the movements and look for any patterns. You should rest," Rose says.

"I'll be at your side for this," Fi objects.

"You need to be fully rested and ready for this," Rose says.

"You forget how much sleep I already had today? I'll be right here," he says.

"You also ran a lot. You should really rest," Rose insists.

"There will be time for R and R, this isn't the time. I'm not moving from this board until we have a location of a possible base," Fi says.

"Okay, you win. We'll look together from different sides," Rose says, walking around to the other side.

After a lot of careful studying, Rose points, "Looks like that right there is a hot spot for them."

"Yeah, just as many leave there go there. That may be a refueler or ammo depot," Fi says.

"Next place to visit?" Rose says.

"I don't like the idea of leaving the base with machines out there," Fi says.

"There's no activity near us, I think we're in the clear," Rose says.

"Then comes the question of how many troops to deploy. Every soldier out of the base is one less defending," Fi says.

"You and I could go alone to check it out. We're the fastest," Rose says. "It would leave maximum people here defending."

"If we're just sending two, why not send two others? Didn't Rand designate some troops as scouts?" Fi says, questioning Rose's idea.

"Do you trust anyone else for this? Do you trust anyone else with me?" Rose asks.

"You're right, these guys aren't soldiers yet," Fi says, taking a deep breath. "Which is why we should all be here."

"We need to gather intel on our enemy. If Aida is still alive we need to know," Rose says.

Fi says nothing, just staring at the board for a moment. "Fine," he says with a sigh. "You and me."

Rose smiles, knowing she won. "You can teach me some of this sneaky survival stuff on the way," she says.

"Alright, you better listen then," Fi says.

"We should really go now," Rose says with a glance to the board, "while there is no activity near our base."

"Not after that run," Fi starts. "We had a long march out there, then ran back."

"I'm fine," Rose insists, trying to act tougher than she is.

"Weren't you training with others while I slept? We'll go in the morning," Fi says.

"Because you're tired," Rose says.

"Because I know this long march out there will be exhausting, and if we need to run or fight we won't have the energy for that," Fi states.

"I could walk all day," Rose says.

"This isn't a casual walk, if we get into trouble adrenaline will exhaust you quickly. We go in the morning," Fi orders.

"Okay," Rose says, "See you in the morning," She starts heading out.

"Rose, I know what you're doing. I do appreciate it," Fi says.

"What am I doing?" Rose asks, turning around annoyed.

"You don't want to feel like a burden, I get it. You think I'm holding you back. This is for both of us," Fi says.

Rose nods, "Good night," and continues to her room.

Recon by Mud

Rose wakes up well rested and gets dressed. She stops by Fi's room with a gentle knock. Then a harder knock. She calls for him, still no answer so she heads down to the courtyard, still no Fi. She sees more training drills with the new guys.

Rose enters the command room to see Fi exactly where she left him, still at that table with another soldier overlooking the map.

"Good morning," Rose says, "Sleep well?"

"Good morning Rose," Fi says, "I did. Got right back here. We're good for our scouting run. There was no activity all night."

"All night?" Rose asks.

"Yeah, got people watching the map at all times now," Fi says.

"Okay, so ready to go?" Rose asks.

"Go get a long coat you don't mind getting covered in mud," Fi says. "And if Havoc had one in my size, please get one for me too."

"Umm, Okay. Are you actually going to be stylish now?" Rose asks.

"I'm always stylish," Fi says.

Rose just gives him a disapproving look.

"Armor is too loud and clunky for a stealth run," Fi says, loosening the straps of his armor and lifting it over his head like a vest. His shirt comes up a bit and Rose notices his abs and gets mesmerized for a moment.

"Armor has saved my life many times, but it's so heavy," Fi says, taking off his cloak too.

"I think this is the first time I've seen you without your armor," Rose says, taking in the view of his muscles showing through his shirt.

"Ah, well enjoy the view, cuz it probably won't happen again," he jokes. "So, long coats," he reminds her.

"Right, stylish trench coats," Rose says, as she leaves the command center and goes to her quarters for a different coat for her and a coat for Fi.

"Wow father, you don't have much style, huh?" Rose says, shifting through the same style coats just different colors. "Brother would've looked good in this, Fi would look better," she says, closing Havoc's wardrobe. "Now, for me. Mother always had good style," she says, opening Helen's wardrobe. "Now, what's a good style for stealth? Oh, black, there we go," she says to herself.

After finding coats, Rose leaves to meet back up with Fi. She finds him by the gate, talking to Filip and some other soldiers.

"Hey Fi," Rose says, handing out the coat she picked for him, disappointed to see he's wearing his armor again.

"There you are," he says, taking the coat from her. He notices a little disappointment in her eyes and asks, "What's the matter?"

"I thought you weren't going to wear your armor," Rose says, disappointed she can't see his muscles showing through.

"I thought about it, we're going into unknown territory with confirmed hostiles. You should be wearing armor too," Fi says.

"Yeah that makes sense," Rose says with a sigh, watching Fi put Havoc's coat over his armor. She smiles when his shirt lifts a bit.

"You'll see me without my armor again," Fi says, comforting her. "Don't worry."

Rose smiles and turns red as she looks away.

"We're going to be out for a while, I was filling them in on everything and leaving the gatekeeper in command until we return," Fi says, as if that interruption never happened.

"Filling them in on what?" Rose asks, looking back to Fi.

"We should start sending out scouts. I'm thinking four man teams at minimum. If there are travelers or other settlements they can try to convince them to join us," Fi says.

"Oh cool. When are they going?" Rose asks.

"After we deal with these machines," Fi says.

"Okay, are you ready to go scout?" Rose asks.

"Yup," Fi says, putting on the coat, "on you gatekeeper." Filip hears his cue and opens the gate for them.

After a little while of walking through mud and checking Fi out in the new coat, Rose says, "You know you look great in that."

"In this?" Fi says, belly flopping in a mud puddle from the huge rain storm the previous night.

Rose is speechless with surprise and confusion. She manages to get out, "What are you doing?" Once she sees him rolling around in the mud.

"Camouflage. That heavy rain left a lot of mud, that will help us blend in," he says.

"You ruined that coat to roll around in the mud," Rose says, judging him. "That's just cold."

"Actually quite warm. Mud traps in a lot of heat, can make a great insulator," Fi says.

"I thought we were going to scout out a possible refueler facility, not roll around in mud," Rose says.

"Cover yourself and let's go," Fi says, throwing a mud ball at Rose.

Rose turns so the mud ball splats against her coat, "hey rude" she says.

"Rose, looks like you got a little mud on you," he says, getting up next to her.

Rose quickly buttons up her coat and looks to see how much mud is on her when Fi just slaps her chest with mud. The slap leaves a muddy handprint on her coat as well as launching a splatter of mud on her arms and face. Rose doesn't move for a moment, then spits out mud.

"You okay?" Fi asks, sounding a little guilty but also trying hard not to laugh.

Rose just looks at him, drops to her knees and digs her hands in the mud pretending to sulk.

"I'm sorry," Fi says, all humor gone. Kneeling down beside her, "I thought that would be funny for-" he gets interrupted by Rose scooping a double handful of mud at him, splattering mud all over his face.

Rose bursts out laughing, "no need to apologize, that was very funny."

"Well," Fi says, spitting mud. "I guess that was kinda funny."

"I can't think of anything funnier than that," Rose says, still laughing.

"I can think of something," Fi says, scooping an arm around Rose and throwing her in the mud pit face first. Fi can't contain his laughter.

Rose gets up on her knees, smearing away the mud from her eyes just to start spitting out more mud. That causes Fi to laugh even harder, his contagious laughter makes Rose start laughing too.

"Okay, now we can go," Fi says, continuing to walk in the direction of the possible fuel depot.

"Really? That's the whole lesson?" Rose asks.

"There may be more later. For now, let's hurry. We wasted enough time," he says, checking his hand drawn map.

"Enjoy the little things," Rose chuckles, then notices his map. "When did you draw that?"

"While you were getting a coat for me. Inside a plastic bag to protect from the elements," Fi says, feeling clever.

After a while of walking, Fi notices a building off in the distance, "That should be it," he says, pocketing his map.

"Great, finally," Rose says.

"Okay, remember, reconnaissance only," Fi says, getting low and watching for any movement.

"I know, not prepared for a fight at all," Rose says. "I only have a pistol and you're actually stylish."

"Follow my lead," he says, once he's satisfied nothing there has moved.

"By your side," Rose says, crouching right next to him.

"Let's move in quick and quiet," Fi says, laying low crouch sprinting.

Halfway across the field, Fi whispers, "drop," and dives face first in the mud with his arms in front of his face shielding it from mud.

Rose watches him and does the same, landing just next to him. "What is it?" She asks.

"Movement," Fi replies.

"This isn't a good spot to be in," Rose says. "We stick out in this field."

"Our coats are covered in mud, as long as they don't focus on us we should blend in just fine," Fi says. "Try not to move, the grass here will break up your outline just enough to stay hidden without moving."

"Right, clever," Rose whispers back.

Fi watches again in the direction he first saw movement until the shadow is gone, "Alright, we're clear, let's go."

"How many did you see?" Rose asks.

"Unclear, just saw a shadow moving," Fi says back.

"So confirmed movement, unknown if it's hostile," Rose says.

"You got it down fast," Fi says smiling.

"It sounds more complicated than it actually is," she whispers back.

"Yeah, sound off, this point on we go in silently," Fi says.

"Silence," Rose whispers back.

They reach the closest building and follow alongside it. They get to the corner and Fi peaks around.

"Big warehouse, not too far, let's check there," Fi whispers to Rose.

Rose follows Fi as he moves from cover to cover, staying low. They reach the warehouse and slowly move to the corner to peek inside.

"A lot of barrels," Fi says, looking in. "Definitely looks like some kind of fuel depot."

"Any machines?" Rose asks, watching the back.

"None that I can see. This must be operated by people. We should bring an assault force in the morning," Fi says.

"So are we good?" Rose asks.

"Yeah, I think so. Small number of people and a warehouse full of combustible liquid. We can mount an assault with this info," Fi says, moving past Rose following their path out.

As the town disappears from sight, Fi and Rose begin to talk.

"That went well," Rose says casually, as a loud bang is heard somewhere behind them followed by a zip going past them.

"Get down!" Fi yells, diving face first in the mud and looking back with his rifle out.

Rose follows quickly, "Was that a gunshot?" Rose whispers with her pistol out.

"See anything?" Fi whispers.

"Nothing," Rose whispers back.

"Let's get down that hill and behind a tree," Fi whispers, motioning to the hill just past them.

"Okay," Rose says, "You first or me first?"

"You first, I'll cover," Fi says.

"Okay, I'm going," Rose says, getting to her hands and knees slowly. She takes another look around to see nothing but a field so she gets up to her feet and rolls down the hill and darts to the closest tree. Upon getting to her feet she hears more gunshots, the bullets impacting all around the tree she's behind. She panics and dives behind another tree getting in the mud.

Immediately after the shooting stopped, Fi followed suit, diving down the hill and getting behind a tree close to Rose, quickly covering himself in mud. His rifle, his face, scooping mud over his legs, then he rolls over stomach down to look at Rose.

Rose imitates what Fi did, covering every bit of exposed skin and laying face first facing Fi.

After what seemed like hours, Rose looks around slowly. Seeing no one, she opens her mouth to whisper to Fi when she hears footsteps nearby. She quickly lowers her face back in the mud.

"Ah, right here," someone says, "I saw two people right here."

"Your rounds all hit the tree," another voice says.

"It was a good backdrop," the first man says.

"Were you trying to hit the tree or a person?" The second man says.

"Perhaps they're in the trees," the first man says back.

"Look, the mud is disturbed. Let's track them," the second one says.

They both move around the trees carefully until they arrive at the tree Rose is hiding behind. "There's no tracks, how could they not leave any tracks in mud?" The first man asks.

"There's disturbance there," the second man says, "Looks like they were running in a hurry and fell. But no tracks after that."

Rose is so scared, she's looking right up the barrel of the first man's rifle. He's facing away with his rifle lowered, pointing directly at her face. She closes her eyes again and tries to calm her mind ignoring what the men are saying.

"Man, I was hoping I'd get a kill on my first run," the first man says.

"Yeah, I hear ya. Let's see how the traps did," the second man says, as they begin to walk off.

Listening to the direction of their footsteps she hears them go back to the clearing and walk out of hearing distance.

Now Rose pokes her head up and looks at Fi, who's already looking at her. "Now?" She mouths without saying a word.

Fi nods, putting a finger across his lips. They both get up slowly and quietly, now standing behind their trees peaking around.

Fi clears the mud from his barrel first, then quickly and silently moves to the next tree in the clearing to look for their attackers. Nothing, they completely vanished. Just like how they were when they shot. Fi moves back to Rose, facing the field.

"Let's go, double time it," he whispers.

"Alright," Rose whispers back, as they attempt to run in deep mud.

"We can't go straight back to base," Fi says, glancing back at their mud prints,

"Any ideas?" Rose asks.

"We should make it difficult to track us, wander a bit."

They run for a while as the sun gets lower and the mud starts to dry.

"Sun is getting low," Rose starts. "Do you think those people were from the fuel depot?"

"Would be quite a coincidence if they weren't," Fi says.

"Yeah, they would've heard the shots if it wasn't them," Rose says.

"Right, these people are a danger to us, we need to act fast," Fi says.

"Will we be prepared enough to hit it in the morning?" Rose asks.

Fi thinks for a moment, "maybe the following morning," he says. "We need to prepare for this assault, come up with a plan, and get you some armor. We'll keep monitoring the map for activity."

"Get me armor?" Rose asks. "Why would I need armor?"

"Did you forget, we made armor out of the machines we brought back from our first assault," Fi says.

"No I didn't forget, I'm usually not in these confrontations," Rose says.

"And now you will be. Remember when the capital was destroyed, you saw me take several shots from a machine. Rand thought I was dead, but my armor caught it," Fi says.

"Right," Rose says, remembering.

"If Rand wore armor he would've been fine when Summer attacked him," Fi says.

"My brother never liked armor, big and clunky," Rose says, repeating what her father and brother always said about armor.

"You could be the only one of your family to not die by a bladed weapon," Fi says, half sarcastically.

"Not cool!" Rose yells, "Don't joke about my family's deaths."

"I'm sorry, that was too far," Fi says.

"Besides, my mother was shot," she says sadly.

"Oh, I must've missed that part," Fi says.

"Yeah, you were unconscious," Rose says, quickly calming down, "must've been that big heavy armor weighing you down."

"Glad to see you got your emotions under control now," Fi says, ignoring the tease.

"Yeah, working on that. Gotta remain focused on the here and now," Rose says, with a deep breath.

"That's good, so Rose, what's with this 'eyo'?" Fi asks. "I heard you say it, I just don't understand it."

"It's my greeting," Rose says cheerfully.

"'Hello' wasn't enough for you? Or was it too much?" Fi jokes.

"I'm just figuring out the kind of person I want to be," she says, shrugging her shoulders.

"And coming up with new greetings is part of that?" Fi asks.

"Why not?" Rose says.

"I mean, no harm, I guess. But just changing your greetings?"

"I'm afraid," Rose blurts out.

"Afraid of what?" Fi says, confused.

"Afraid of being alone and forgotten," Rose says.

"Rose, I will always be here with you. You've got nothing to fear," Fi says.

"I've heard that a few times now, no one that has said that to me is still here, still alive. Except you," she says.

"And yet you keep finding people that are willing to stay with you. People come and go, enjoy the time you have with them, remember them, never forget those that helped you get to where you stand today," Fi says.

34

There's a moment of silence between the two, as Rose remembers her family. "No one will want to remember my family for what they did. Remembering me will remind them of what my parents have done, what my brother did. I can't let them disappear. I need to keep their memory alive. Everyone says hello there or hi, if my greeting is similar enough to recognize as a greeting, but different enough for people to remember, then they won't forget me," Rose says.

"Wow, that's deep. Don't worry, as long as we're all around, people will remember you. And they will remember you for all the good you have done," Fi says, putting an arm around her shoulders. "I promise you, I will never forget you."

"Thanks Fi," she says, going in for a hug.

"Well it's a long walk back, we better pick up the pace," Fi says, looking back for anyone on their trail.

Target Practice

Rose and Fi arrive back at their home base just after the sun sets.

"Would you fine people like in?" Filip says, opening the gate.

"Why yes, thank you Filip," Rose says.

"Eyo," Fi says.

"Eyo to you too," Filip replies.

"See you in the morning Rose," Fi says.

"Morning? You think I'm going to go to sleep covered in mud?" Rose says back.

"I mean, you can change, you don't have to sleep with mud all over you. I just mean I won't bother you until the morning," Fi says with a pause. "So, see you in the morning."

"Are you not going to shower first?" Rose asks.

"Are you?" Fi says smirking.

"Probably not," she says.

"So you're going to your room for the night. I'll see you in the morning," Fi repeats again.

"Yeah, I guess," she says annoyed. "See you in the morning," as they part ways and go to their separate rooms.

As Fi turns away to get to his quarters Rose notices something about his armor.

"Fi," Rose calls out, getting his attention just before he walks down a hallway.

"Yes?" He says, turning around to face her.

"Turn around," she asks, waking closer to him.

"Uh, okay," Fi says, tiredly.

"You were shot," Rose says, putting her finger in a hole in the back of his jacket.

"Oh was I?" He asks, turning around and taking off the muddy jacket and tossing it at Rose.

"Hey," Rose says, annoyed, tossing back the coat.

"Can't remove my armor without taking off the coat first," Fi says, tossing the jacket to the ground to take off his armor. Holding it in his hands, he turns it over to notice the scratch Rose pointed out. "Oh, I was," he says casually.

Rose is speechless at how casually Fi just reacted. Then says, "You were shot and that's your reaction?"

"Well I'm not hurt. No use reacting about it if I can't change anything about it," Fi says.

"You were shot, you could've died," Rose says.

"No I have armor, that's what armor does. Saves me from bullets," Fi says.

"Maybe that armor idea isn't so bad after all," Rose says.

"Maybe not, and tomorrow you'll decide on it," Fi goes to turn around, stops half facing Rose, "We've said good night a lot tonight, so we say it once more?"

"Good night," Rose says with a smile.

Fi turns around and says, "goodnight," back. He picks up the jacket and takes it with him.

Rose gets to her room, takes off the muddy coat and just hangs it on the back of her door. *Don't want that to get other things dirty*, she thinks. Then goes to her drawer and pulls out a washcloth and wipes the mud off her face. She lets out a sigh when she sees the amount of mud that made it onto her clothes under the coat. "This will need to be washed in the morning," she says to herself, taking off her belt and setting it on her nightstand. She takes off her muddy clothes and throws them in the corner by the door. She's about to put her pajamas on when she feels how much mud is in her hair. "Great. Not getting in bed like this," she says with a sigh.

She finds one of Helen's nightgowns and clean pajamas then sneaks out to the bathroom to shower. After drying off and getting into pajamas that are a little big, she walks back to her room and crawls on top of her bed. She's out fast.

She wakes up in the morning after a long night's rest. She yawns and stretches, then goes to her wardrobe to decide what to wear for the new day. Then remembers her muddy clothes from yesterday. "Oh yeah, I should wash those," she says out loud to herself. She decides to wear a black shirt to contrast her white trench coat. And of course, her gun belt.

She brings all the dirty clothes back to the bathroom to clean them. She fills up a bucket with water and soap and begins scrubbing.

When her clothes are dry, she brings them to her room and hangs them on her window frame to dry.

Then she then heads out to the courtyard to see Fi already working on something.

"You really don't sleep much, do you?" She asks.

"Good afternoon sleepy head," Fi says back.

"It's not that late," Rose objects, looking up to see the position of the sun.

"Yeah, anyway, I need your measurements," he says, holding up a measuring tape.

"For what?" It's then that Rose notices what's on the workbench, a plate of metal, looks like it came off a machine.

"For your armor," Fi says, gesturing to the workbench.

"Okay, I see that now. What do you need?" Rose asks, reaching for the measuring tape.

"Jacket off, I'll do it," Fi says, getting up and facing her.

"Okay," Rose says, taking off her jacket and resting it on half on the table hanging off so it doesn't touch the ground. "What's first?"

"Shoulders," Fi says, getting behind her and placing the measuring tape from one shoulder across her back to her other shoulder. "Okay," Fi says, stepping beside her to lean over his workbench to write something.

"Chest," Fi says, then looks at her awkwardly. "Let's, um. I'll get behind you, just put it in the right place," he says awkwardly.

"Right place?" Rose asks, sharing in his awkwardness.

"You know what I mean," Fi says, getting behind her, reaching over her head and draping the tape loosely across her chest.

"I don't think I do," Rose says, confused.

"Just put it at the part that sticks out the most," Fi says, wanting this to be over.

"Okay," Rose says, "that's all you had to say," laughing.

"Okay," Fi goes around and writes again. "Now, just below the last measurement."

Realizing that he's uncomfortable with this, Rose teases him a little more. "Which measurement?" She asks.

"The last one we just did," Fi says, kinda annoyed.

"Right, and where was that one?" Rose says, maneuvering the measuring tape all over her torso.

"You're making this difficult," Fi says, with a sigh.

"You're difficult," Rose says back.

"Just, under your boob okay," Fi says, finally giving up.

"Oh, that's just below the last measurement we took of my," Rose says.

"Just get the number please."

"Okay," Rose says with a victorious grin.

"Finally. Okay, now from your collar bone to the bottom of your ribs," Fi says, after writing down the last number.

"Okay, I understand the shoulders and the chest, but why ribs?" Rose asks. "You're not going to make me that feminine style armor. I want as much protection as you," she says sternly.

"Armor ends at the ribs," Fi says. "My armor ends at my ribs. It's a heavy metal, it just needs to cover the vitals."

Rose looks at Fi's armor, yup, it ends at the bottom of his ribs. "But don't you want the most protection? Why don't you cover more?" She asks.

"It's protection versus mobility. If you cover your whole torso you can't bend over, you can't crouch, you're severely limited," Fi says. "Armor over your chest, thighs, and joints is the best compromise."

"Okay, that makes sense. Just, don't give me boob armor," Rose says.

"Okay, really?" Fi asks sarcastically.

"Really, I don't want it," Rose says.

"You realize that doesn't even work. Besides, you're too flat anyway," Fi says jokingly. "Your armor will look just like mine, just smaller."

"Okay, first of all, rude, second, when will it be ready?" Rose asks.

"Depends, do you want the joint pieces too, or just the chest?" Fi asks.

"I'll be fine with just the chest," Rose says.

"Like half a day to get this into shape then a few hours making a vest to hold it," Fi says, sitting down at the workbench.

"Okay, I'll practice a bit then," she says, grabbing her coat.

"Practice what?" Fi asks.

"Shooting, maybe join in on some drills," she says.

"Great, I can't wait to see how your aim is," Fi says. "Do you workout too?"

"Yeah. Push-ups every morning and most nights," Rose says, flexing under her coat.

"That's good, very good," Fi says.

"I may not say anything or acknowledge you, but I'm always listening. My brother taught me the most when he wasn't teaching," she says.

"Wow. Impressive. But I doubt you're always listening," Fi says, teasingly.

"Okay, most of the time. You can be very annoying sometimes," Rose teases back.

"Sometimes? Yeah, you definitely don't listen that much then," Fi says back.

"Sometimes I like your annoying, sometimes you get too annoying," she says.

"Anyway, I need to finish this," Fi says with a big smile. "Go ahead and do what you said you were going to do now, I'll find you when this is done."

After hours of drills with her soldiers, Rose is back at the range, watching the sun get low as she loads mags between firing. Her shooting is getting better.

Fi calls out as he gets within ear shot, "Rose, your armor is done." He makes sure to call out before he gets to close, nothing worse than startling someone with a loaded gun.

Rose turns around to see Fi with his rifle slung over his shoulder. "Hey, glad you could join me."

"And miss you shooting?" Fi jokes, "wouldn't miss it for the world."

"Great, well I'm just about ready to shoot another mag," Rose says, slamming a mag into her pistol.

"Indeed my timing is impeccable," Fi says, putting on a spare set of ear protection. "Call it when you're ready."

"Range hot!" Rose yells, disengaging the safety then shooting. The targets she set up are just empty bottles and small rocks. Each shot destroys a target. Every shot lands. Once she gets the infamous *click* she engages the safety and drops the empty mag calling out, "range cold."

"Very well done," Fi says, taking off the ear protection as Rose does the same.

Rose doesn't know pride so she doesn't know how to respond to that. She just smiles and thanks him.

"Did Rand teach you that?" Fi asks. "I don't recall you ever using a gun… You're an amazing shot."

"I watched how he did it, then I practiced it myself," Rose says.

"How are you with a rifle?" Fi asks, grabbing his rifle from his back to hold it out to her.

"Not as good. I don't get why my shots aren't as accurate with a rifle," Rose says.

"Show me your technique, I'll see if I can offer any tips," Fi says, still holding out his rifle. After watching Rose struggle with accuracy, Fi gives some help with her technique.

"Okay, that's better, you're hitting more than you're missing now," Fi says, after Rose fires another barrage.

"Okay, are rifles just harder?" Rose asks.

"Usually, no, just different. It's heavier to compensate for the recoil, and bigger for both hands to steady it," Fi says.

"I'm still much better with my pistol," Rose says, setting the empty rifle down on the table in front of her.

"It just takes some practice. Let's see what you got with your pistol," Fi says, stepping back.

"Alright," Rose says, picking up her pistol and loading another mag into it and quickly decimating every target.

"Yeah, you're a natural," Fi says. "That's better shooting than me with a pistol."

Rose smiles, "it just feels better."

"Yeah I bet. That would be great for human targets in case any raiders find us. But when it comes to the machines, only the armor piercing rifle rounds will do the job," Fi says, picking up his rifle and putting it on his back.

"Are you going to shoot now?" Rose asks.

"Not just yet," Fi says, loading a mag for his rifle.

"Okay, I wouldn't mind another demonstration of rifle shooting," Rose says.

"I do make a great model, don't I?" He says, inserting the loaded mag into his rifle, then slinging it to his back again.

Rose blushes, "An excellent model."

"Oh, then let me come back with a target to model," Fi says with a smirk before dropping the ear protection and walking away.

Rose is annoyed and shocked at how sudden Fi just left. "Well, I guess I'll just keep shooting then," she says to herself, loading in another mag.

"Alright, here it is," Fi calls out as he approaches Rose again.

"Oh, that's my armor?" Rose asks excitedly, engaging the safety and setting down her pistol.

"Yup, I'm going to demonstrate how bullet resistant it is," Fi says, holding it out.

"I'll pass. I don't want to get shot," Rose says, declining the armor piece with a confused look.

Fi returns the confusion, "I'm not going to shoot you."

"I don't want to risk it. I'll take your word for it," she says, again declining to wear the armor.

"I'm not going to shoot it while you wear it," Fi says laughing. "I'm handing it to you so you can set it out at a distance we can shoot some rounds at it."

"You know that makes a lot more sense. Okay," Rose says, finally accepting the armor. "Oh, this is heavy."

"It's two pieces of metal shaped to your size, wrapped in thick fabric. It's going to be kinda heavy, but you'll get used to it," Fi says.

"Okay," Rose says, running out down range to place it down propped up by a big rock. She runs back to Fi at the table.

"Alright," Fi says, holding up a partially loaded rifle mag, "three normal rounds, three armor piercing, let's see how they do." Fi loads the mag into his rifle and takes aim. He notices Rose picking up her pistol and aiming. "Range hot!" He calls out, disengaging the safety and firing into the armor.

After their mags empty, they both set their weapons down. Upon seeing the other setting their weapon down, they take off their ear protection together.

"Alright, let's see how well I did," Fi says.

"If it's broken you're gonna have to make a new one," Rose says.

"If it's broken it means our armor is useless and we're screwed," he jokes.

"Well, let's hope," Rose says back.

As they approach the target they notice no holes and a lot of scratches going from the center to the outer edges. With three noticeably deeper scratches. "Those would be the armor piercing rounds," Fi says, pointing to the deeper scratches.

"Wow, now that's impressive," Rose says. "So how does this armor stop AP rounds when these are what killed the machines?"

"The armor plates block our armor piercing rounds, but there are places between the armor plating that the armor piercing rounds can destroy," Fi says, clarifying. "The frontal plates, what our armor is made of, is impenetrable to small arms fire. The lesser armor around the rest can be penetrated by these AP rounds."

"Okay, that makes sense. Do I put it on now or," she pauses for him to answer.

"I would clean it, the 9mm rounds mostly just exploded on impact. So just a rinse off really, then maybe paint it or something," Fi says.

"Paint it?" Rose says, waiting for him to elaborate why.

"You know, personalize it. Whatever you want," Fi says.

"Ah, I gotcha," Rose says, picking up the armor just right for the sun to reflect into her eyes. She looks up to notice the sun getting lower in the sky. "When are we hitting the fuel depot?"

"You got your armor and more practice, so let's go in the morning," Fi suggests. "Better go get some sleep."

"Alright, are you going to sleep too?" Rose asks.

"I will make appropriate arrangements for tonight, then I will get some sleep," Fi says.

"You know I can take care of that stuff too, you don't have to bear the weight of the world on your shoulders alone. We're doing this together," Rose says.

"I know. I just," Fi pauses trying to find the right words.

"You think I can't keep up just because I'm a girl?" Rose asks.

"No, not at all," Fi says, going back to looking for the right words.

"So it's because I'm young," Rose says.

"No, would you just wait. I'm trying to put my thoughts into words and it's not working," Fi says.

"It's rather boring," Fi starts. "You need to keep up on the training."

"So it is because I'm young," Rose says, annoyed.

"No, inexperienced, that's the word," Fi says. "You don't have the experience yet."

"I can't get that experience without experiencing what it is you're doing," Rose says.

"Experience isn't taught or given, you have to go through it yourself. Right now you need to focus on yourself, once you can take care of yourself, you can start taking care of others too," Fi says.

"My father always taught us the other way around, so taking care of each other is the first thought, not the second," Rose says.

"Look where that got Rand," Fi says. Fi fails to notice the moment of silence where Rose's rage builds.

Rose slaps Fi looking furious at him.

"I'm sorry, I could have worded that better," Fi says, taking a moment.

"Yeah, you should have," Rose snarled.

"The only thing he cared about here was you. You were his whole world, so when he was putting you first he was holding the weight of the world on his shoulders. He thought of you both first which led him to do bad things for you. I want to make sure you are strong enough on your own that you don't need anyone. Once you're in a place of complete independence, then you can start helping others," Fi says.

Rose finally understands, it wasn't her brother that went crazy, it was bad teachings that led him down that road. She opens her mouth to say something, but nothing comes out.

After a moment, seeing she's not saying anything, he adds, "You have to put the others' needs before your own, not instead of your own."

"I get it," Rose finally mumbles. "I get it now."

"I'm glad you do. Now, go get some rest," Fi says, in a gentle voice.

"Okay," Rose says, walking back to the gate. She looks back expecting Fi to be following, but he's just sitting at the table with his back to her, looking down range.

Rose gets in her room in silence. Thinking about her brother. She sets the armor on the floor by her dresser and changes into her nightgown and climbs into bed haunted by thoughts of her brother and how they were taught.

What Went Wrong?

Rose wakes up ready to take on the day. She picks out not a cute outfit, but a badass one. She puts on her armor over a red shirt, then her white trench coat over it. "Yeah, I'm ready," she says, posing in the mirror.

There's a knock at the door, "Rose, you ready?" It's Fi.

"Yup, everything in place?" Rose calls back through the door.

"Yup. Everyone is arming up and getting into formation," Fi responds.

She opens the door to leave to see Fi there, leaning against the wall. "Good morning," she says.

"Good morning," Fi says. "Destruction and mayhem await, he jokes."

"Can't wait," she says.

"Love your new style," Fi says. "That red underneath, is that symbolic?"

"What?" Rose says, looking down at her clothes.

"The red underneath the armor and white. Like a fire burning deep, armor like a shield of loved ones, and the white coat is purity of who you are on the outside," Fi says, droning on.

"What are you talking about? I just like these colors. White with red looks good," Rose says.

"Oh, okay. Yeah, that does look good," Fi says.

"Don't read too far into what isn't there," Rose says with a joke.

"Yeah, you aren't an easy read," he says back. "Anyway, let's get to the courtyard."

"Alright, let's go," Rose says, following as Fi leads. "Rand loved red," she says to herself.

"Are you coming?" Fi asks, glancing back.

"Yes," Rose says with a smile.

Fi waits for Rose to catch up then reaches for her hand. When he grabs her hand, she instinctively grips back.

Rose looks down at their hands and blushes, she looks at his face to see how he's taking it.

Fi is grinning ear to ear and red all over. Rose could practically hear his heart rate standing beside him, or was that her own heart beating so fast?

They walk down to the courtyard and as soon as they see their troops in formation waiting for them, Fi pulls his hand back. "Let's do this," he whispers to Rose as he speeds up.

Rose is a little disappointed Fi withdrew his hand, just a few minutes of holding his hand felt like an eternity. Snapping out of it, she moves faster to catch up again.

"Alright everyone," Fi says, moving to the front of the soldiers. "Our mission is a fuel depot. Scouts confirm there are human targets there. Rose and I were ambushed by sniper fire out there, we believe the snipers to have come from there. Rule of engagement is if it has a weapon, drop it. These people may be slaves, so we may be taking prisoners, they may even join us as some of you have. Our Intel shows machine transponders going in and out frequently, so there may be machines around too. Primary objective is to destroy the fuel containers and clear all combatants. Secondary objective is to find more intel on the machines. We will be splitting up into two fireteams. One will be Overwatch with our big guns, the other will be an infiltration team. Once our big guns are in range, the infiltration team will move up just outside the facility. Overwatch will fire onto the fuel depot, hopefully eliminating any machines there. Any questions?" Fi says, ending the briefing.

"Wait, there have been machine sightings?" Rose asks.

"We've been tracking the transponders," Fi says.

"Okay, have you already given everyone their role?" Rose asks.

"I did last night. This was just a recap for them and to let you know the plan," Fi says. "Jeremy is leading the Overwatch team, you and I are leading the infiltration team.

"Okay," Rose looks at her people to see armor similar to hers and Fi's on most of the troops. "I see most of us have armor, why not everyone?" Rose asks.

"Not enough material. The more machines we destroy the more armor we can make," Fi says. "Majority of the infiltration team has armor that will deflect rounds from the machines. The rest have armor that will at least catch a few rounds."

Everyone is silent. "Okay, you have your orders, let's move out!" Fi calls out, marching towards the gate

"Hoorah!" Everyone shouts, following suit through the gate.

They all arrive at the open field, "Fire on those warehouses," Fi orders. Once the Overwatch team sets the elevation they give Fi the signal. "Charge!" He shouts, as Overwatch fires over their heads, arcing their shots to hit the warehouses.

The infiltration team spreads out as they charge, watching for movement ahead. Without warning, the entire area explodes. All the buildings they could see, just engulfed in flames. The blast sends a shockwave that knocks everyone down.

"Hold! Hold!" Fi shouts getting up quickly, trying to get everyone's attention, but they're all too shocked by the large blast. Ears ringing, vision blurry.

Everyone stops, some in awe, some in terror at the sight. Eventually they start looking around at each other and notice Fi is trying to regroup them. Everyone's ears are ringing. The fire burns very fast, taking everything down with it in minutes. Once all the fuel is gone, the fire disappears as suddenly as it started.

"Everyone on me!" Fi calls out.

"Fi, what happened?!" Rose calls back. "We were supposed to bring survivors home, not kill everyone!"

"I think this was more than just a fuel depot, but a fuel mine," Fi says.

"That would explain why the ground blew up," Oscar says.

"This was not the plan," Fi says softly, "I'm sorry. New objective: find survivors. Secondary objective remains, learn what we can about the machines."

The Overwatch team moves up with the infiltration team and sets up a defensive line where they entered.

They go through in formation, block by block, seeing everything destroyed. Rose gets flashbacks to her city, then the capital. "We did this," Rose says out loud as they pass some destroyed homes with cooked bodies inside.

"We had no way of knowing," Fi says, trying to comfort Rose.

They pass a building to see a charred adult body holding two child size bodies. That scene breaks Rose. *That could've been her, Rand, and James.* She falls to her knees in tears. "We did this," she repeats.

Fi gets down next to her and lays an arm across her shoulders, "It was a mistake."

"We did this!" Rose yells, forcing his arm off her and standing up. "We were supposed to stop this from happening, not cause it!"

"You guys go ahead and continue searching, we'll catch up," Fi says to the squad.

Fi sits back with Rose while the remainder of the troops search what's left.

"Sir, we found the transponders. Parts of machines are decorated around some of the buildings. These guys were able to take on the machines too," Oscar says.

"The perfect allies and we killed them," Rose says. "That's enough," Fi says to Rose, "We had no way of knowing the entire settlement would explode like that."

"Let's not plan to kill everyone we meet, Rand," Rose says, comparing Fi to Rand.

"You were with me on reconnaissance, you didn't say anything then, so stop now," Fi says sternly.

"We need to make contact first, before we decide to kill everyone," Rose says.

"Those snipers ambushed us, there was no way to introduce ourselves peacefully," Fi says.

"No way of knowing now, seeing how they're all dead," Rose snarks.

"Rose, enough," Fi snaps. "You think this is emotional only for you? It was my plan! I gave the order to fire! I feel it too! Getting emotional on the battlefield gets people killed! Now fall in line now."

"Sir, we should head back to Home Base now. We've gone over everything, no survivors," Oscar says.

"Very well," Fi says with a sigh, "Jeremy inform Home Base we're on our way."

It's a long silent walk home. Not a word is said.

"Open the gate!" Fi calls out, once they're in earshot.

"Welcome home," Filip says. "Doesn't look like we lost anyone, what's with the sad faces?" He asks.

"No survivors," Fi says, as Rose just walks past without a word.

"My lady, you alright?" Filip asks.

"She just needs some time," Fi says, watching her go straight to her quarters.

"Dang, what happened?" Filip asks Fi.

"We fired on the warehouse and the entire settlement blew up," Fi says, as everyone enters their base.

"Damn. Like, the entire thing, not just smoke?" Filip asks.

"The settlement must've been on top of a fuel line, the shot at the warehouse set everything around ablaze," Fi says. "No survivors."

"Oh. I can see why she's taking it so hard then. How are you holding up?" Filip asks, closing the gate as the last person enters.

"Shaken, but I'll manage," Fi says.

"You can open up to us, you shouldn't keep everything bottled up like that," Filip says comforting Fi.

"Thanks, but I can't feel this just yet. Can't let my emotions control me," Fi says.

"Letting them build up gives them power over you, eventually they will control you. Do what Rose is doing, if you don't want to be around others just let it out in your quarters," Filip says.

"No," Fi says, starting to get irritated, "I need to focus it."

Fi moves to the training dummy, which is just a big piece of a machine they scavenged held up by a piece of wood. Fi turns to the guard shack to see Rand's sword. He takes it and begins swinging at the scrap metal. Swinging harder and harder with every hit, shouting with every swing. Letting all his anger out through violence.

A loud noise of metal shattering as Fi looks at the scrap metal in shock. Seeing deep slashes and dents. He starts to feel amazement until he looks down at the sword to see it half the size. The sword is what shattered, not the machine part. Rand's sword is broken. Fi feels horrible for breaking it. He sets the half he's holding back at the guard shack, then picks up the broken blade half, cutting his hands, he stabs it into the ground right next to the training dummy. Without a word, Fi enters the living quarters and goes to his room.

Enjoy The Little Things

After a few hours alone in her room, Rose gets hungry. Not wanting to potentially see Fi or anyone for that matter, at the mess hall, she climbs over the wall to get to the fruit trees just outside of the walls to the north. She gathers an armful of pears and apples then sits down leaning against a tree facing the horizon as the sun sets. *What a beautiful view,* she thinks to herself.

"Just like brother always said, take time to enjoy the little things," she says, holding up a pear, trying to take her mind off of what happened outside the walls. "Thank you for your sacrifice, brother," she says, taking a bite. These trees have the sweetest, juiciest fruit she had ever tasted. She watches the sun set, feeling peace. The most relaxed she had felt since her city blew up. She dozes off for a bit.

Rose wakes to the sound of leaves rustling behind her. She stretches and calls out, "Over here Fi." But there's no response. She gets to her feet and looks around with a yawn, the forest is pitch black. No light, no movement. She turns back to her base to see it silhouetted with lights from inside. "I can hear you, I know you're there. Come on out," Rose calls out, facing the darkness once again. After more silence she begins to panic, feeling alone, her breathing kicks up. She tries to ignore it, *maybe just a small animal.* She turns to go towards her home. After a few steps she hears more movement behind her. Trying harder to ignore it and not be afraid, she continues walking away faster. The more she resists the fear, the stronger it gets. She starts shaking, the fear overpowering her, she takes off in a full sprint, adrenaline dumping making her run faster.

She makes it to the gate heaving out of breath and calls to Filip, "OPEN THE GATE!"

Filip looks confused as he looks around frantically until he spots Rose. "Oh, didn't realize-" he stops, opening the gate. "...Everything alright, my lady?"

"There was someone watching me," Rose says between breaths.

"Where?" The soldiers on night watch all move on top of the wall looking out with their weapons ready.

"I don't see anything," one says.

"It's too dark, I can't see anything," another says.

"Out in the fruit trees, someone was watching me," Rose says, finally catching her breath. They scan the area, the only sound is Rose's heavy breathing.

"My lady, you shouldn't go outside alone. No one should," Filip finally says.

"Yes... I think you're right," Rose says. She heads back to her quarters, passing the guard shack, something reflects light in her eye, she turns to see a broken sword. She gets closer to see it's Rand's sword. Someone broke her brother's sword.

All the guards there are silent, they know who broke it.

Rose doesn't say a word, just takes the sword with her to her quarters. After leaning the fractured sword against her night stand, she notices how dirty her clothes are and decides just to lay on top of her bed for the rest of the night.

She falls asleep quickly as she is exhausted physically and mentally, the mental exhaustion taking a heavy toll she has a dream.

It Begins

    Rose is awoken to sounds of gunfire and shouting. She runs to the balcony in haste to look over and see several soldiers trying desperately to hold the gate shut, while the rest are on top shooting out. In her haste, she realizes she left her holster in her room. She runs back and grabs her belt and checks her pistol ammo; full mag. She looks over to her night stand to grab her brother's broken sword, it's not there. She looks around the room, noticing nothing else has changed. Putting on her armor she runs outside.

    Upon reaching the wall, she sees Fi up there with his rifle.

    "Fi!" Rose shouts, climbing the stairs to the wall carefully.

    "What are you doing here? You're safer in your room!" Fi shouts over the sound of the gunfire.

    "I can take care of myself!" Rose yells back, ducking on the wall, peaking over the cover.

    "I can't protect you down here!" A familiar voice calls out.

    "They're breaching the gate!" One soldier calls out. As the gate flies open beneath them.

"I got 'em!" The familiar voice calls again, jumping down and drawing her brother's sword. He makes quick work of the attackers. Taking out multiple with a single swing, parrying others for quick followup strikes.

Rose looks back over the wall to just see hooded figures, some with guns others with swords. She takes aim, calms her mind and slows her breathing. She takes her first shot, head shot. First time she has shot someone, second time taking a life. She was close enough to watch his head explode making her nauseous. She looks to another, slow breathing, head shot. She shoots another thirteen rounds, every shot hitting exactly where she aimed it. She ducks down when she gets the empty click, "I'm out!" She calls over to Fi.

Fi ducks behind cover and looks around at his feet for more pistol ammo. "Here!" He shouts, standing up to kick a box over to her. Upon kicking the box, Fi gets shot three times. Once in the upper arm, twice in the chest. The shock causes him to freeze for a moment before falling back off the wall.

"FI!!" Rose calls out in pain, watching his limp body smack the ground hard.

Rose slams a fresh mag into her pistol and peaks over the wall to see how many enemies are out there. She panics in disbelief seeing there's no end. Just hooded figures charging as far out as she can see!

"Fi! I will kill you all!" The familiar voice yells in rage, the clanking from the swords gets louder as the swings get heavier and faster.

Rose looks down to see how many are left, that's when she finally recognizes that voice; it's Rand! He's alive!

"Sister! Go back inside! It's not safe!" Rand yells, upon seeing her on the wall.

Rose blinks and rubs her eyes. He's still there, that is her brother.

"Get inside!" Rand yells again.

"You need my help!" She objects.

"I can't protect you up there!" Rand yells yet again.

Rose starts looking around frantically to come up with a plan, that's when she realizes everyone is dead but her and Rand. Bodies everywhere. Her breathing kicks up, her hands shaking, she's panicking.

Rand looks back to see Rose still on the wall, "get inside! I will protect you!" He shouts again.

Rose looks down to him, "we're the only ones left," she says in shock, too quiet to be heard. "It's happening again," she begins to repeat to herself. "It's happening again."

"Rose!" Rand shouts, the viciousness of it snaps her out of it. "Get inside now!"

"We'll go together!" Rose shouts back loud enough for him to hear it.

"That's the plan, you go first! I'll cover you!" Rand shouts.

"Okay!" Rose shouts, running down the stairs from the wall. As soon as she reaches the bottom the fighting completely stops. No gunfire, no swords clashing, no shouting, no noise. Complete silence. Rose turns around to see all the hooded figures are gone. The alive ones and the dead ones. All that remain are her fallen friends, her brother. He's still facing the wall.

Rose races towards Rand ready to cry on his shoulder, once she reaches him, he starts bleeding in the abdomen. She goes around in front to see a sword stabbing him. Her eyes widen as the tears flow, "brother! No! Come back! " She calls out to any entity that would listen.

"Sister, this is your fault," Rand says, reaching down and pulling the sword out.

That's when Rose notices it's his own sword. But it's broken now. Broken the way Fi broke it on the training dummy. But the sword wasn't broken when they were fighting here. Rose is too distraught to hear his first words.

"If you stayed inside I could've protected you," he says, falling to the ground.

"You needed me here," Rose says in tears. "I could protect you while you protect me."

"If you stayed where it was safe this wouldn't have happened," Rand says bleeding out

"Why are you saying that?" Rose demands.

"You killed everyone," Rand says. "You killed everyone. We were only trying to protect you."

"Wait, this isn't that bad!" Rose says, "I can fix this, let me get my first aid kit," she gets up to run inside but gets called over by Fi.

"Rose, over here," Fi says.

Rose is in shock, looking over at his mangled body, "You're alive?" She asks in disbelief.

"Rose, come here," Fi calls out again.

Rose hurries to Fi, "How are you alive?"

"I'm not. You did this. I was just trying to protect you," Fi says.

Rose notices how much blood is around him, he shouldn't be alive. "I don't need you to protect me," she says back, kneeling beside him.

"You do," Fi says. "Look at you. You need us! You got us killed!" Fi says.

Rose is in a complete panic. She doesn't know what to do. She doesn't understand what happened. She closes her eyes and covers them with her hands. "This isn't happening, this can't be happening!" She says to herself.

"Oh this is happening," another familiar voice says. "And there's nothing you can do to stop it."

Rose opens her eyes to see Fi is gone, no blood left behind. She looks over to Rand's body, gone. Every body disappeared again.

"Over here sweetie," the voice says again.

Rose looks in the direction of the sound to see all of her people alive, but on their knees facing her. Behind them is Summer.

Rose rubs her eyes and looks again, yeah, everyone is alive and Summer is behind them.

"Let's get started," Summer says, stabbing Rand in the back. He calls out in pain, as Summer twists the blade and yanks it out fast. The sudden burst of pain leaves Rand almost paralyzed until Summer kicks him forward.

"Brother!" Rose calls out, reaching for her pistol, just to realize she doesn't have her gun belt. She doesn't have her armor either. She looks back to see Summer holding her pistol.

"I said I'd stab him in the back if I got the chance," Summer says. "And since you shot me," she pulls the trigger, shooting Rand in the back. "Karma's a bitch." She then turns the pistol on the others, executing one at a time.

"Brother!" Rose calls out, springing to her feet and running to Summer.

Summer points the pistol at Fi, "One more step and your boyfriend dies too!"

Rose stops immediately in her tracks. She can't lose him too. She can't be alone. "Why are you doing this?" Rose asks.

"I only had one person that ever cared about me, ever wanted to protect me. Everyone seems to want to protect you, and you fight them on it. You know what it's like being alone? Having no one to protect you?" Summer says.

"I don't need anyone to protect me!" Rose finally yells.

"Do you know what it's like being alone?" Summer repeats.

"No," Rose answers.

"You will," Summer says, shooting Fi in the back of the head, splattering blood onto Rose. "You will."

Rose looks Summer in the eyes, the anger, the hate, it startles Summer. Startles her enough for Rose to get an opening, she leaps at her like a wild animal, clawing, punching, slashing at her face. Summer is quickly subdued, but Rose isn't done. She grabs the collar of her shirt to lift her head up and punches her. Over and over again. When there's nothing left to recognize Summer, Rose grabs the knife she stabbed Rand with and stabs Summer in the heart.

Starts gently, then leans on it to get the blade all the way through.

"No one kills my brother but me!" Rose shouts menacingly. She stops and thinks about what she just said. Those weren't her words. *No one kills my brother but me?* She thinks. Those aren't her thoughts, those can't be her thoughts.

Rose looks back to her brother to see him sitting up smiling, "You're just like me," he says.

Rose looks down at her hands to see them covered in blood. Then looks at what's left of Summer in fear of herself. She looks to Fi to see him sitting up too.

"I knew you were just like him," Fi says, smiling.

In that moment of absolute fear, Rose wakes up.

The room is silent… black.

"Please… that can't be me."

Not His Fault

There's a knock at her door, "Rose you in there?" Wiping her eyes, she hears a voice she recognizes but can't place the name. *How long have I been crying?*

Again, the knock startles her, she's still panicked and doesn't answer.

"Rose?" The voice calls again, this time worried.

"Yeah... yeah I'm here," she calls back.

"Just want you to know, Fi is really worried about you."

"I'm fine!" She calls back, annoyed, getting off of her bed.

"My lady, I'm worried about you too. Do you want to talk?" He asks.

"Talk about what?" Rose asks back, now changing into clean clothes.

"Whatever you want, whatever helps," he says.

"And if I don't need help?" Rose calls back, deciding against wearing a coat.

"Then something to help me," he says. "If you don't need help, would you help me?"

Rose opens the door to see Jeremy. "You're not who I was expecting," she says surprised.

"We all care about you, some just don't know how to express it," he says.

"Well, what is it you need help with?" Rose asks.

"I know you're the boss and you'll do what you want, but please be safe. No one knew you were outside the walls last night," Jeremy says.

Rose sighs.

"Please my lady, you were scared of something out there and no one could help."

"Why does everyone feel the need to protect me?" Rose asks, frustrated. "Filip already said that to me."

"We all want to protect each other. I know you're capable, we all want to be safe," Jeremy says.

"I'll talk to Fi about a buddy system," Rose says, annoyed.

"Look, Rose, we really care about you. You are a better leader than your parents. You actually care about us, just want you to know we do care about you too," Jeremy says.

"Oh, thanks," Rose says, at a loss of words.

"What happened yesterday with the assault wasn't your fault. Nor was it Fi's," Jeremy says, "anyway, want you to know that the first set of scouts went out this morning."

"Oh yeah. Are they staying out until they find people or is it a day at a time thing?" Rose asks.

"Fi says it's at the discretion of the scouts. But that they need to decide before they go and exactly where they're going," Jeremy says.

"Did we get more radios or are they going out there blind?" Rose asks.

"I'm training others on the radio so we can have a radioman out there without me going every trip," Jeremy says.

"That's good. So who's got the radio?" Rose asks.

"Didn't have time to train anyone, Oscar just said he would lead the first scouting patrol without the radio. I'll have someone trained to use it once they're back. I'll probably go on the next one," Jeremy says.

"That sounds great, thank you for telling me," Rose says, happily.

"No problem, my lady. I was on my way to report to Fi, but decided to check in on you first."

"Well you definitely fixed my mood, so thanks. I'm going to see Fi now too," Rose says.

Jeremy turns to leave, and Rose follows him to Fi who's in the command center.

Rose waits for Jeremy to give his report on the scouts before approaching Fi. She sees Fi and pictures him dead, just like her dream. She's afraid of losing him and herself.

"We found another settlement, this time we're going to introduce ourselves before we engage. Rose, I would like you by my side again," Fi says.

"I'll always be by your side," Rose says.

"That's a relief, thank you," Fi says, taking a deep breath. "I was worried about last night."

"I'm fine. Things happen, that wasn't our fault," Rose says.

"I'm sorry about how I handled it," Fi says.

"I'm sorry I blamed you," Rose says.

"Something you should know, I was relieving my anger with a sword last night," Fi starts, Rose looks at him wide eyed. "I broke it," Fi finally says. "I broke Rand's sword. I'm very sorry."

Rose feels all the sadness from when she discovered the broken sword, and more now for knowing it was Fi. That sadness quickly turns to anger. She looks Fi in the eyes, she sees the pain he feels, the remorse for his actions. Seeing that in his eyes makes that anger turn back to sadness. She opens her mouth to speak but nothing comes out. Finally she gets control of her emotions and says, "It's okay. I forgive you."

That moment was an emotional rollercoaster for Fi. He could see her sadness, then saw her eyes fill with anger. He was so worried about what she would say, until she finally spoke. "Oh good," Fi says with a sigh of relief. "Okay, now that that's over, on to business?" Fi asks.

"Onto business," Rose repeats.

"Okay, so according to the map," Fi says, gesturing to the big map, "the machines didn't touch this settlement, so it could be abandoned or it could be aligned with them. Or it's just so small Aida didn't consider it a threat."

"Are we taking any troops as back up?" Rose asks.

"I don't want to. Not after what happened last time," Fi says. "We need allies, allies are built on trust. If we show up with a lot of firepower it may scare them."

"Will we be armed?" Rose asks curiously.

"Of course we will be, we don't know them yet, trust is built over time not instantly," Fi says.

"Great, when do we leave?" Rose asks.

"At first light," Fi says, with a smile.

"Will you be sleeping before then?" Rose asks.

Fi gives a familiar look and asks, "Probably. Do you want to organize everything so I can sleep?"

"Sure," Rose says happily, excited to be involved. "Wait, what needs to be organized if it's just us two?"

"My sleep schedule," Fi says with a laugh.

Rose looks annoyed, "so you're not going to let me actually do anything."

"Okay, that was a joke," Fi says. "Are you a light sleeper? You're going to be the one everyone brings questions to tonight."

"I can sleep light," Rose says.

"Okay, I'm trusting you on this," Fi says.

"I won't let you down," Rose says confidently.

"Rose," Fi pauses, his face sucking all the joy from the room, "I know what that sword meant to you. I'm really sorry."

"I know you are. It means a lot to both of us," she says, hanging her head low.

Fi holds out his arms for a hug, Rose jumps in immediately.

Right here, this moment. In his arms is the safest she had felt since the capital. The warm embrace brings a tear to her eye. Peace.

This hug brings out his weakness, emotions. By letting in that peace and feeling of being loved, he feels the opposite that he's been burying all these years. He starts tearing up too. This moment is the best moment he has had since he lost his parents.

After an unusually long hug, they break away, both wiping away their tears. "Thank you, I- I needed that," Fi says, as he starts walking out of the command center.

"Where are you going?" Rose asks, noticing his bandaged hand.

"To sleep," Fi says, turning around backpedaling, "Goodnight."

"Um, goodnight?" Rose calls back unsatisfied. She was expecting more, something about that hug. She watches him leave, "Wait, it is morning."

"It's afternoon, and I didn't sleep at all. Now that you're awake you can run things," Fi says walking out the door. It closes behind him.

"Should I be glad you're giving me this responsibility… or upset you're leaving me like this?"

Sighing, Rose says aloud to herself. "Well, there's always stuff to do."

I'm in Charge

Rose steps outside to the courtyard, *train or run things?* She thinks to herself. *I need some experience of being in charge*, she decides to head to the well first.

The well is right in front of the mess hall, a stone circle surrounding the spring with a bucket and rope.

Rose leans over the stones to look inside, water. Good. *Okay, now to the mess hall.*

She walks in the mess hall to see people eating. *Let's find out where this food comes from and how I can help out.* She ventures to the back to talk to the ones that make the food.

"Eyo," she says, greeting the people making the food.

"Oh, my lady, what a surprise," the chef says, "What can I do for you?"

"I would love to know how you guys get the food to prepare here," Rose says.

"Gardens," the chef says, "You've seen the fruit trees, we have vegetable gardens too."

"That's good, constant supply," Rose says. "Who tends to them?"

"I do. I pick them and cook em," he says, sitting down at a table.

"Well, thank you for everything you do," Rose says, joining him at the table.

The chef smiles, "You're very welcome," he says.

"How are we doing with food?" Rose asks.

"Well before, uh. Well, under Havoc, we collected food. It was more, we ate like kings," he says.

"I know. My brother didn't like that. But that's in the past. We're here now," Rose says. "We've had meat every now and then, where'd that come from?"

"Mostly the food storage. We grow the necessities and have a lot of other stuff stored for special occasions or emergencies. Oh, and snares," he says.

"Snares? Like hunting traps?" Rose asks.

"Yes, I set it and catch something like once a week, usually pretty small," he says.

"Awesome, where are they?" Rose asks.

"In with the fruit trees, disguised pretty well I might add," he says with pride.

"Oh, I didn't notice them," Rose says.

"You go out there alone?" He asks.

"Yeah actually," Rose admits.

The chef's face drops, "don't go out there alone, especially after dark," he says.

The sudden tone shift makes Rose on edge, "Why not?" She asks.

"I've been hearing things," he says.

"What kind of things?" Rose asks.

"Unnatural things. Some of my traps get sprung but there's nothing inside," he says.

"You think something is watching your traps and taking your food?" Rose asks.

"Someone," he corrects. "Someone has been taking our food."

"Why haven't you told anyone? I had no idea about this," Rose says.

"My lady, I tried. I didn't think anyone would believe me," he says. "You probably think I'm crazy just like the rest."

"I believe you," Rose says.

"Oh that's so good to hear," he says, happily.

"I was out there last night, I heard footsteps close by, I called out and nothing," Rose says.

"I'm glad you're safe," he says.

"Yeah, I ran back to the gate and some of the night watch went out looking, they didn't find anything," Rose says.

"We aren't safe here, even right in our own damn walls," he says.

"No one goes out alone until these people are dealt with," Rose says.

"You want to find a buddy for your garden?" Rose asks.

"Two won't be enough," he says.

"Unfortunately that is all we can spare right now. We can spread out the guys on the walls for a better view. You can tell them when you're going out and they can help keep watch from the wall," Rose suggests.

"That would be great," he says. "When are we getting more people?" He asks.

"I don't know," Rose says.

"Well there has to be more people out there, we just need to find them and hope they're friendly," he says.

"That we do," Rose says.

"So is there anything else?" He asks.

"Why don't we go to the garden and you can show me where your traps are," Rose says.

"What a great idea," he says.

"What's your name?" Rose asks, as they leave the mess hall.

"Jerry, but most people just call me chef," he says.

"Alright, Jerry, let's go see these traps," Rose says with a smile.

As they pass by the guard shack by the gate Rose stops and asks, "Jerry, do you have a weapon?"

"No," Jerry says, walking on.

"Do you want one?" Rose asks.

"No," Jerry responds.

"Uh, okay," Rose says, catching up with him at the gate.

"Hey Filip, we're heading to the fruit trees," Rose says.

"Be safe my lady," Filip says, opening the gate. "My, is that the chef? I don't think I've seen you outside the mess hall. Did little Rose here drag you out?" Filip asks.

"I usually go out just before dawn, before everyone has breakfast, to get everyone breakfast," Jerry says as a matter of factly.

"My apologies, I didn't mean to come off rude," Filip says.

"We're going to inspect the traps and see the garden," Rose says, changing the topic before it becomes an argument.

"Sounds like fun. Be safe you two," Filip says, as Rose and Jerry leave.

Jerry doesn't say anything on the walk, it's rather awkward for Rose. She wants to talk, but the feeling is just awkward silence.

"Ah, my fruit trees," Jerry finally says as they enter the grove.

"They really are the best fruit I've ever had," Rose says.

"You know it," Jerry says back with pride. "The fruitiest and juiciest you'll ever find."

"Definitely," Rose says.

"I set the traps out randomly," Jerry says.

"Do you remember where?" Rose asks.

"Of course I do, I left markings for them," Jerry says.

Rose understands why he's always alone now. He's not great with people.

"Okay, what are the markings?" Rose asks.

"You see that tree?" Jerry says pointing in a manner Rose can't see. "You see that tree?" He says, pointing at other trees. "See that tree?" He says, turning around and pointing at more trees.

"I don't see anything those trees have in common," Rose says, expecting a ribbon or a series of broken branches of some kind.

"Anything in common? They're all trees," Jerry says.

"I mean anything out of the ordinary to mark a trap," Rose says defending herself.

"If the markings were out of the ordinary, everyone would find them," Jerry says. "They're hidden, that's how traps work."

Rose is getting annoyed at how he keeps talking down to her.

"Here's the first one," Jerry says, pointing at a pile of leaves on the ground.

"Doesn't look disturbed," Rose says, making an observation.

"That's because nothing disturbed it. Let's go to the next one," Jerry says.

"Lead the way," Rose says, sounding annoyed.

"You keep following, I'll keep leading," Jerry says walking on towards the next trap.

Rose rolls her eyes and follows behind him. After checking a few undisturbed traps they finally find one that looks active.

The dirt around it is all kicked up and the rope is untied. Someone took the catch.

"Damn. This is what I was worried about. Traps getting untrapped," Jerry says.

"Someone untied it," Rose says to herself, looking around for further evidence.

"Good observation," Jerry says.

Rose ignores his comment, "there's some blood here, small drips," she says, looking at faint dried drops. She follows the trail to a small rock, "looks like the creature was killed with a rock before being taken."

"Yeah, that's what blood means," Jerry says.

"We need more people so we can get some patrols through here," Rose says.

"Waste of resources," Jerry says.

"You don't think we need food?" Rose asks.

"Well, my lady, I'm sure you were raised with the best food. Whatever you wanted whenever you wanted, but some of us are satisfied with an already massive food storage and unlimited fruit," Jerry says.

"That food storage isn't unlimited, it's going to run out eventually. Especially winter time," Rose says, staying calm.

"Let's get back, I have things to do," Jerry says, turning to the wall.

Yeah, I don't even want to see the garden, Rose thinks to herself.

They both make it back to the gate when Jerry turns around to face Rose. "Rose, I'm sorry, I'm not all that good with people," he says. "I tend to just say what's on my mind, I hope I didn't bother you too much."

Rose smiles, "no worries, I understand. Is that why you are always alone?"

"Yeah, I kinda prefer it. See you around," he says, walking back to the mess hall.

Rose looks up to the sky, the sun is still high and bright. "So what now?" She says to herself. "Good on food, good on water, let's check the wall," she says going to the gate. Remembering what her parents taught her as the essentials: water, food, shelter.

"Eyo Filip," Rose calls out as she gets to the gate.

"Eyo my lady," Filip says back. "Off on another thrilling adventure?"

"Nothing planned for today, just checking on the walls," she says.

"Not to worry my lady, these walls aren't going anywhere," Filip says, leaning over to give the wall a good slap.

Rose chuckles, "I'm more talking about weak spots or openings with no guards."

"Ah, well your parents made sure these walls were as sturdy as possible. But with less manpower we could have more open spaces than before," Filip says.

"Okay, I'm going to have a look up there and try to space people out for maximum coverage," Rose says, approaching the gate.

"Alright, thanks for being thorough," Filip says, turning back around facing outside the wall.

Rose gets to the stairs leading up and remembers her dream. She sees Fi at the top shooting. She sees her brother at the gate on ground level with his sword. Rose stops in her tracks, *what a nightmare*, she thinks. Shaking her head to shake loose those thoughts, she heads up the stairs.

Rose reaches the top of the wall and looks out to enjoy the view. Instead she's hit with a flashback of memories escaping the capital. Her heart skips a beat as she closes her eyes, trying to relax. She opens her eyes to see the hooded figures from her dream charging at the gate. Her heart beats faster. *This isn't real.* She freezes in place, looking out at her nightmare.

Filip notices Rose standing petrified on the wall and cautiously walks over to her, looking from her to where she could be looking. "My lady," he says, getting right up next to her, looking where she's looking. He sees nothing, just a nice view.

His words snap Rose out of it, she turns to Filip, then back over the gate. Everything is clear. Everything is calm, except for Filip. Rose starts taking deep breaths to calm herself.

"My lady, what is it?" Filip asks, almost panicking.

"Nothing," Rose says, turning away from him.

"Nothing? You were terrified, you don't scare. I need to know," Filip says.

"It's nothing," Rose says, not even facing him.

"Rose, if there's a security risk I need to know. This isn't personal if it affects everyone's safety," Filip demands.

"You don't make demands of me!" Rose yells, quickly facing him, she didn't mean to be so quick to anger, but her adrenaline levels are still high.

"If everyone here is in danger I need to know. You can't keep it to yourself," Filip says, lowering his voice from yelling to casual conversation.

"It's not about anyone," Rose says, still in a yelling tone.

"What did you see?" Filip asks. "Was it someone outside the walls? The one that has been following you?"

"It was a dream! Just a dream!" She yells. At this time more people are coming out to see the commotion.

"A dream about what?" Filip asks.

"Nothing," Rose says. "It was a dream. It doesn't concern you or anyone's safety." Rose turns back around and continues around the perimeter of the walls.

Rose is aggravated, she can't focus on the wall. Somehow, just acknowledging the dream made it real. Made it a problem. No longer just her thoughts. Her breathing kicks up again. She looks around to see she's alone, she wanted to be alone. But now she feels alone.

Still unable to focus with her anxiety getting the best of her, she decides to go to her room. Not a word is said as she passes Filip, she doesn't even look at him. She doesn't make contact with anyone. She goes inside and sits on her bed. All she can think about now is losing Fi and her brother again.

She takes off her coat and hangs it on her wall and proceeds to punch it. She hits straight through the fabric and hits the wall, making a loud noise and hurting her hand. The pain helps turn that fear of loss into anger, and that anger into strength. She hits it again, harder. Again. And again. She's giving this coat all she has.

For my brother, she hears a crack with that hit, *for Mother... for Father,* a quick crack. *For Fi!* Her fist punches through the wall, splitting the wood. She looks at her hands to see them covered in blood.

Rose doesn't give it a second thought, she moves to the center of her room and starts doing push-ups.

Rose notices her coat swaying on the wall, she checks her window, closed. After a moment it gets pulled to the side from beyond the wall.

There's a man there, looking in.

"What do you want?" Rose calls out.

Upon seeing Rose, the coat gets moved back. "Sorry my lady, just checking on you," he calls out.

"Well I'm fine, you can go," Rose says, still using that anger as strength.

"Were you attacked?" He asks through the wall, "There's blood on you."

"Someone put a wall behind my coat," Rose says, going back to her push-ups.

"Do you need anything?" He calls once more.

"I need to be alone," she answers back.

After an exhausting workout, Rose wraps her hands and puts on her nightgown before passing out.

It's the same nightmare. Again. Filip is at the top of the wall this time.

Larger World

Knock, knock, knock,

"What is it?" Rose calls through the door, getting out of bed.

"Oscar, my lady," Oscar says. "Just got back from scouting."

"Anything to report?" Rose snaps, opening her door.

"Yes, and I was told to report to you that Fi is sleeping… Sorry if I woke you," Oscar says, noticing Rose is in pajamas.

"Fi and I run this place together. What do you have to report?" Rose asks.

"We made contact with some travelers. They didn't want to tell us where they were headed or where they came from, but we did share some stories," Oscar says.

Rose's face lights up when she hears that. "That's wonderful! What kind of stories?" She asks.

"Well they were really hesitant to share much, so we just told them about how we destroyed the machines, you, Fi, that stuff," Oscar says.

"That's really good. Do you know which direction they were going? Maybe we can try to find their destination and negotiate an alliance," Rose says.

"Possibly, I'll leave a note on the map in the command center. I'm ready to rest," Oscar says.

"You definitely deserve that rest," Rose says. "Good night."

"Good night, my lady," Oscar says back as he turns to head to his quarters.

Rose smiles and closes her door. "Oh man, I can't wait to tell Fi in the morning," she says out loud to herself as she gets back to bed. The good news now overshadows her nightmare.

There's a knock at Rose's door that wakes her. She sits up rubbing her eyes, "What is it?" She calls out followed by a yawn.

"First light, let's go," Fi calls through the door.

"First light? What's- oh yeah, I'm getting dressed," she says, rushing out of bed to get dressed.

"Long night?" Fi asks.

"Nothing I couldn't handle," Rose says back, now picking a coat.

"Great, it actually felt weird sleeping that much. I didn't like it," Fi says.

"Seriously?" Rose asks, confused as she opens the door.

"Seriously," Fi confirms. "I just felt like there were a million things I should be doing."

"You stress too much," Rose says.

"Well we're pretty much all that's left to get everything back to normal. That can be stressful," Fi says.

"Would be half as stressful if you let me carry half the load," Rose says, leading the way out to the courtyard.

"Got to test the water before you jump," Fi says cryptically.

"I think I did well," Rose says.

"I was told you had trouble yesterday," Fi says. "What was the problem?"

"Trouble?" Rose responds.

"Part of trust is knowing you can be relied on, the other part is knowing you tell me what's going on," Fi says.

Rose lets out a sigh, "what did you hear?"

"Someone I trust told me you saw something… it scared him. You blamed it on a dream then got super hostile towards him," Fi says.

"I had a nightmare, that's it," Rose finally replied, not looking up.

"What kind of nightmare?"

"The kind I want to forget," Rose says aggressively.

"What was it about?" Fi asks.

"The more it's brought up, the longer I remember it," Rose growles back.

They go on a few paces more.

"Listen. The more it controls you, the less I can trust you," Fi says back. "Rose, talk to me. Please."

"I can't. I just need this to go away," Rose says, getting more frustrated.

He thinks. "That bad, was it a memory?" Fi asks. Seeing her shake her head he tries again, "Did you see people you care about die?"

Rose's eyes fill with tears. She finally makes eye contact with Fi.

"That's rough," he says, holding out his arms to embrace her. "I can't live with seeing people I care about die once, I can't imagine seeing it twice."

"Not just twice," Rose says crying in his arms, "Over and over."

"Oh, I'm so sorry. I'm still here." He gives her some time before talking again, "is this about your fear of ending up alone? Was this caused by leaving you alone?" He asks.

"I don't know," Rose says, tears slowing down.

"Well at least it's only at night," Fi says, trying to comfort her.

"No," Rose lifts her head up to look him in the eyes, "I see them during the day too."

"Who's them?" Fi asks, moving a hand from her shoulder to her cheek to wipe away the last of her tears.

"You, my brother, everyone here," Rose pauses for a moment. "Even Summer."

"Even Summer? You still care for-" Fi asks.

"She killed you," Rose says, cutting him off through the tears.

"Hey, try not to let that get you down," Fi says, forcing a smile. "Would that dream and frustration have anything to do with the hole in your wall?"

Rose remembers punching her coat, "Oh. Yeah," she says casually wiping her face.

"Well I think some time outside the walls will help, don't you?" Fi asks.

"Yeah," Rose agrees, looking down still, "Getting claustrophobic here."

"Then let's go enjoy our time outside," Fi says smiling.

Without thinking, Rose gets on her toes and gives Fi a quick kiss. They both stare into each other's eyes with a smile, then turn red. Both trying to come up with something to say, still gazing into each other's eyes.

"We- we should head out," Fi finally says.

"Right, right. We should be heading out now," Rose says, stumbling through her words.

There's an awkward silence as they break the hug and walk together to the gate.

"I think you're doing a great job leading," Fi finally says, breaking the silence.

"You think so?" Rose asks with a smile.

"Yeah, I heard you took charge, went over our food, water, and walls," Fi said. "Perhaps we should get the troops to start reporting to you too."

"Well, Oscar did report to me, he told me he made contact with others," Rose says.

"That's great!" Fi says, "tell me everything."

"The people they met were travelers, not a settlement or anything. They told them stories about us," Rose says.

"What stories?" Fi asks, as they get to the gate.

Filip, seeing that they're in the middle of a conversation, doesn't say anything, just smiles and opens the gate.

"How we destroyed the machines of course," Rose says as they leave. "What's wrong with telling stories?"

"That's great and all, but did they mention Rand or your parents?" Fi asks.

"Why do you always dwell on the negative?" Rose asks.

"We have to be careful about what is said outside of our walls. If people hear about what your family did, and that you're still a leader, it may shake trust," Fi says.

"I'm sure our scouts are only saying good things about us," Rose says. "And even stories about my family are great."

"I know, I know, legendary warriors. Rand saving all of us, but people tend to judge others based on their mistakes," Fi adds.

"That is true," Rose says with a sigh. "Mistakes only define you if you let them."

"Failure doesn't define us, it's how we respond to that failure that defines us," Fi says, wording it better.

They continue walking, discussing scouting and meeting new people.

"That looks like it's it," Fi says, pointing in the distance to what looks like some farm. "Looked a lot bigger on the map."

"So what's the play here?" Rose asks. "This is my nice coat."

"No mud, we aren't hiding anything. Let's scout it out from a distance then move in," Fi says.

"Alright, let's go."

They walk around to see it's a collection of many farms, all that look deserted.

"All the buildings are standing, nothing looks blown up. I don't think machines came here," Fi says.

"Maybe everyone's indoors," Rose suggests.

"A place like this with no lookouts?" Fi asks back.

"Yeah, I'd expect to have seen someone by now," Rose says.

"Well, let's knock on a door then," Fi says, moving in.

As they get closer Fi notices something shiny reflecting light in his eye, looking down he sees a bullet casing.

"That can't be good," Fi says, kneeling down to inspect the casing only to see more in the grass. "Looks like a firefight broke out."

"That means people did this," Rose says, saddened.

"That's why we didn't see anyone," Fi says, sadly.

"Do you know how long ago?" Rose asks.

"Can't get much from just casings. Let's check for survivors," Fi says, grabbing his rifle from his sling.

Rose draws her pistol too, "Just in case," she says.

"Just in case," Fi says back.

As they search they notice bullet holes all over doors and windows. The first building they enter they see bodies on the floor with blood everywhere. Rose immediately gags and vomits outside.

Fi is visibly distressed, but tries to help Rose anyway, "you alright?"

"I feel sick," she says, holstering her pistol and leaning against the side of the building.

"You never get used to that smell," Fi says, holding her hair back.

"It's not just the smell," Rose says, "these people were murdered."

"You want to wait outside while I search the buildings?" Fi asks.

"Yes please. I can't take it," Rose says.

"Okay, I'm going back in," Fi says, letting her hair down.

"Be careful," she says back.

Fi goes back inside to inspect the scene. No weapons, no casings. These people didn't fight back. They couldn't fight back. He moves through the rooms seeing bullet holes going through from the front. He enters a bathroom to see a body curled up in the tub. The blood splatter is at a downward angle with the bullet lodged in the tub. He looks down to see a single casing. Fi fills with rage, this was a massacre! He leaves out the front door to meet up with Rose.

Rose sees the anger in his face, "What did you see?" She asks

"These people were executed. We need to find out who did this and stop them," Fi says.

Rose is in shock, "Who would do such a thing to unarmed people?"

"We need to stop them," Fi repeats.

"We need to send out more scouts," Rose suggests. There's too many places for just the two of us to find."

"Yeah, we have sent out three sets so far, they need to warn others about people like this," Fi says, in agreement.

"Are we going to check every building?" Rose asks.

"Whoever did this already did," Fi says. "It would be a waste of time. Seeing this just enrages me."

"You're certain they checked each building?" Rose asks.

"I saw someone curled up in the tub with a bullet through his head and one casing in the room," Fi says. "They went room to room executing them."

For a moment Rose doesn't believe it. Then the shock sets in as she sees he isn't lying.

"So, what do we do?" Rose asks.

"Before we head back, there are more settlements in this direction," Fi says, pulling out his hand drawn map then turning his attention to the position of the sun, "looks like we got time."

"Where is it?" Rose asks.

"It's some small buildings hidden in a clearing in a forest," Fi says, walking back to the treeline to check the map he made.

"Okay, hopefully it'll be different," Rose says.

"It will be. I feel it," Fi says back.

The settlement is surrounded by woods, sneaking up on it was easy. As they get to the clearing, they stop and watch from the treeline, "There it is," Fi says.

"They're surrounded by trees but they don't have any walls? That's dumb," Rose says.

"Major security risk, they have all the resources they need, but do they have the manpower is the question," Fi says.

"So we're just going to scope things out from the trees?" Rose asks.

"Yup. Not a good idea exposing ourselves until we know what we're up against," Fi says back.

"Right, let's move together," Rose says.

They move around through the trees looking between the buildings for movement or signs of life. Nothing. There are no signs of life at all.

"Okay, I guess this has been abandoned. We should go in to see if anyone stuck around just in case," Rose says.

"Yeah, big place, think we should split up?" Fi asks.

"Split up?" Rose repeats, "why would we want to split up?"

"I want to get home before the sun goes down, I'll start here at the entrance, you go around back. We can meet in the center," Fi says

"I don't like that idea at all," Rose replies.

"Do you doubt yourself?" Fi asks. "I've seen you in action, both armed and unarmed, you're good."

"It's not that," Rose says.

"You need confidence," Fi says. "You're the strongest person I know. You've grown past Rand."

Rose sighs.

"I'm afraid of being alone... I still can't take it," Rose says, feeling empty.

"Oh," Fi remembers her nightmare and how it might've started from being alone. He thinks for a moment how to address her fear. "I can't think of any other way to move past this fear except facing it head on," he finally says.

"Not like this," Rose objects.

"Of course, let's do this; we start together at the entrance and split off at different intersections. We'll only be one block away and mostly remain in view," Fi says, grabbing her hand.

"I don't like that," Rose says. "But I'll do it," she says reluctantly, taking a deep breath.

"You are incredibly brave," Fi says, looking fondly at her.

"Let's go," Rose says.

"Alright," Fi responds, "I'll keep to the left, you keep to the right," he says, releasing her hand.

"Alright," Rose says, following Fi as he heads towards the entrance.

They sprint from the treeline to reach the back of the first building.

Fi moves to the far corner to peek into the street, "Clear, I'm crossing," he says before running across the street. Fi looks back to Rose, she smiles back. He points down the street and Rose nods. Then they both round their buildings to move to the next for concealment.

Rose goes into the building she just passed, it's empty. Only rusted bed frames and rotten wood furniture. She pokes her head out to see Fi, already outside of his building waiting for Rose. She shakes her head and moves to the next building paralleled by Fi.

The fear of abandonment is causing Rose's hand to start shaking. "I can do this," she says to herself. "I'm not alone." Going into the next building causes her anxieties to worsen. Her shoulders start shaking along with her hands. "I can do this," she repeats, "I'm not alone." The front door shuts abruptly and Rose lets out a small scream as she jumps around with her pistol out. The room is completely dark. The shaking gets so bad she almost drops her pistol.

The fear, the darkness, it's setting in. She can't take it anymore and just charges the way she came in, luckily hitting the door and not the wall.

She makes it outside in the light, struggling to breathe. She looks across the street to see Fi isn't there. She remembers seeing everyone she cares about dying. The hollow feeling grows, she drops her pistol and grabs her wrist tightly trying in vain to stop the shaking. She falls to her knees, "I can't do this," she says between heavy panicking breaths. "I need you, Fi," she looks up to see Fi still isn't there. She closes her eyes.

She hears Rand's voice, "I'm proud to be your brother. Father would be proud of your bravery."

Then Fi's voice, "You're the strongest person I know. You've grown past Rand."

The shaking stops as she remembers who she is and what she's been through. She opens her eyes and looks up to see Fi still isn't there. With the burst of courage she got from her memories she grabs her pistol and runs across the street to Fi's side. There she hears what sounds like fighting. She can't place which building it is, with adrenaline overruling her fear, she begins checking all the buildings until she finds where the sound is the strongest. A large circular building echoing every sound, she rushes over seeing an open door.

Rose sees Fi and another man, both badly injured, still desperately trying to hit the other.

"Fi!" Rose shouts, running closer. "Get away from him!" She yells, aiming at the unknown assailant.

"Take the shot!" Fi says, on the ground between heavy panting and coughs. "Shoot him!"

Rose looks at the crumpled mess of the man that beat up Fi on his knees, she's unable to pull the trigger.

"Shoot him!" Fi yells again.

"He's unarmed," Rose says back.

"He's the one that executed those people!" Fi says, coughing up blood. "Put him down!"

Rose points her pistol to the man's head, uncommitted with her finger off the trigger.

"Do it!" Fi yells again.

Rose stands frozen, her memories of lost friends, and her sense of inadequacy still fresh in her mind.

Their mysterious assailant seizes the moment, "I'll make you a deal. You don't look like a killer, so let me go and you can leave with your boyfriend."

Rose stares deeply into this man's eyes, trying to find the courage to take the life of an unarmed enemy. She looks back to Fi, the anger sets in. This man did that to Fi, this man executed dozens of people, she scowls at the man and slowly moves her finger to the trigger. She's all ready to pull the trigger. Then she thinks of her brother again, "never take a life out of anger." She saddens and removes her finger from the trigger. There's a moment where no one says a word.

Then several others swarm around them, all armed and aiming their weapons at Rose.

"Just in time," the man says, as one of the men gets up next to him to inspect his wounds.

"Don't! He has to die!" Fi yells again.

"Do I have your word?" Rose asks the man.

He nods, "safe travels."

Rose looks back to Fi, then to the man, then to her surroundings. She engages the safety and holsters her pistol and stares blankly back at the man, waiting for him to call off all of his people.

"Let them go," he says, as everyone else lowers their weapons to a low ready stance. Another person walks to the man's side picking him up.

Rose pulls Fi to his feet, but he is unable to stand and falls into her. He is heavy, Rose struggles to support his weight.

"Next time I see you, we'll have a more civilized talk," the man calls out to Rose as she walks away with Fi leaning against her.

"You should've ended him," Fi says angrily.

"You know why I didn't," she says back, saddened.

"He's going to come after us," Fi says, "you better be ready for it."

"We'll manage. We can catch him after you heal up," Rose says.

"And if he doesn't surrender? He has more people than we do," Fi argues.

"Killing in combat is one thing, executing an unarmed and injured enemy is wrong," Rose says defensively.

"He executed a lot of people, he doesn't follow your rules. Next time I see him, I'm going to kill him," Fi says.

"My brother said never to take a life out of emotions. Calm your mind and-" Rose gets interrupted by Fi.

"Your brother knew when to kill and when to spare. This guy is one we kill. If he finds out where we live, he will destroy everything we have built," Fi says.

"The only time Rand spared an enemy was when I got through to him," Rose says. "We need to double our defenses and maybe add patrols."

"Patrols would only leave less time for training. Anyone got close and saw patrols they would know we're close by," Fi says, disagreeing. "Let's just get home to discuss this further."

"Okay. You'll be fine in a few days," Rose says.

Once they're in the cover of trees, Rose puts Fi down to administer first aid to him.

Fi and Rose manage to make it back to Home Base after many long hours and many more breaks.

"Open the gate!" Rose calls out, nearly out of breath.

"What happened?" Filip asks, opening the gate.

"We were attacked, Fi is stabilized, but still needs medical attention," Rose says, as guards come out and help Fi inside. "Thank you," she says, falling to her hands and knees in exhaustion.

"You alright, my lady?" One asks, holding out his hand to Rose.

"I'm fine," Rose says between breaths. "Just exhausted."

"Let's get you some water," he says, still holding out his hand.

"Thank you," Rose says, taking his hand.

He picks her up and takes her to her quarters, as another meets up with them there with a large jug of water.

"Thank you," Rose says, taking the jug, "Both of you." She takes a drink then lays down on her bed. Her eyes close involuntarily.

Not Again

    Rose is just waking up when she hears the sound of gunfire and shouting. She runs to the balcony in haste to look over and see several soldiers trying desperately to hold the gate shut, while the rest are on top shooting out. She reaches for her holster and draws her pistol, checking her ammunition; full mag. She runs outside to help defend her home.
    Crossing the courtyard she sees Fi on top of the wall with his rifle, bandaged up and leaning against the top of the wall to stand.
    "Fi!" Rose shouts, climbing the stairs to the wall carefully.
    "What are you doing here? You're safer inside!" Fi shouts over the sound of the gunfire.
    "I'm not leaving you out here!" Rose yells back, ducking on the wall, peaking over the cover.
    "I can't protect you down here!" A familiar voice calls out.
    "They're breaching the gate!" One soldier calls out. As the gate flies open beneath them.
    "I got 'em!" The familiar voice calls out, jumping down and drawing a sword. He makes quick work of the

attackers. Taking out multiple with a single swing, parrying others for quick followup strikes.

Rose looks back over the wall to just see the man that nearly killed Fi, some with guns others with swords. She takes aim, she tries to calm her mind and slow her breathing. She takes her first shot and hits the man in the head. She was close enough to see his head explode, she feels proud of that shot. She looks to another to see it's the same man. Confused, she slows her breathing, head shot. That's when she starts to realize, they all have the same face. Everyone out there is the man that nearly killed Fi. She fires the remainder of her mag, striking many more, every shot hitting exactly where she aimed it. She ducks down when she runs out of ammo and gasps, "I just killed the same man fifteen times."

"Make it sixteen!" Fi says, leaning up to kick a box over of ammunition to her. Upon kicking the box, Fi gets struck three times. First shot in his cheek, others in his chest. His body goes limp as he falls backwards off the wall.

"Fi!!" Rose calls out in pain, watching his body smack the ground hard head first.

Rose slams a fresh mag into her pistol and peaks over the wall to see how many enemies are out there. She panics in disbelief seeing there's no end. Just people that look like that man charging as far out as she can see!

"Fi! I will kill you all!" The familiar voice yells in rage, the clanking from the swords gets louder as the swings get heavier and faster.

Rose looks down to see how many are left, she sees Filip in a puddle of his own blood, not moving. She looks to the last man standing and recognizes that as her brother.

At this point Rose realizes she's having the same nightmare as before.

"Sister! Go back inside! It's not safe!" Rand yells, upon seeing her on the wall.

"This isn't real!" Rose objects.

"I can't protect you up there! Go inside now!" Rand yells.

"This isn't real! You're just a dream!" She yells back, looking at Fi's crumpled body that no longer has any gunshot wounds, but just beaten to death, similar to how she found him the day before.

Rand looks back to see Rose still on the wall, "get inside! I will protect you!" He shouts again.

Rose looks down to him, "none of this is real! It's not happening," she begins to repeat to herself. "It's not happening."

"Rose!" Rand shouts, the viciousness of it snaps her out of it. "Get inside now!"

"This isn't real!" Rose shouts back loud enough for him to hear it. Upon shouting, everything stops as if time itself froze.

Rand slowly turns his head to Rose, "I'm not real to you?" He asks.

The man he's fighting, the face of the man that nearly killed Fi, then stabs Rand in the chest with his sword.

Rand, not even reacting to the stab, holds eye contact with Rose and says, "so this isn't real to you."

"This isn't real," is the only thing Rose is able to say, trying desperately to stay in control of her emotions through total chaos around her. She closes her eyes for a moment, "wake up, this is just a dream." She opens them to see once again all that remain are her fallen friends and her brother.

Rose turns her attention to Fi this time, seeing him beaten to death. She knows this isn't real, but it looks so damn real she cries anyway. She turns back towards her brother to see he hasn't moved yet, still standing with a sword sticking out of him, just his head following her around. Rose walks over to her brother.

"Sister, this is your fault," Rand says, reaching down and pulling the sword out.

That's when Rose sees it's his own sword. Broken, again.

"If you stayed inside I could've protected you," he says, falling to the ground.

"Stop this, it isn't real," Rose tells her brother that's bleeding out. She's at the brink of crying again. Seeing her brother again.

"If you stayed where it was safe this wouldn't have happened," Rand says, bleeding out.

"Why are you saying that?" Rose demands.

"You killed everyone," Rand says. "You killed everyone. We were only trying to protect you."

Rose closes her eyes, trying to wake up again. "This isn't happening, this isn't happening!" She repeats to herself.

"What makes you so sure this isn't happening?" That voice, she recognizes it.

Rose opens her eyes to see everybody disappeared again.

"Over here sweetheart," the voice says again.

Rose looks in the direction of the sound to see all of her people alive on their knees facing her. Behind them is the man that nearly killed Fi.

"Let's get started," the man says, shooting Rand in the back. He calls out in pain and falls forward.

"Brother!" Rose calls out, almost forgetting it's a dream.

"Sparing me was a bad idea," the man says, "you know I killed those people." Killing her people one by one, pausing occasionally to humiliate her, "You saw what I did to your boyfriend." Two more fall, "You still let me go," he stops at Fi.

The man points his pistol at Fi's head, "you shouldn't have gotten involved."

Rose stops immediately in her tracks. She can't believe this isn't real. "Why are you doing this?" Rose asks.

"Why do you live in a walled city with armed guards that do everything you tell them?" The man asks.

"I don't need anyone to protect me!" Rose finally yells, remembering that's what the nightmare is about.

"Power," the man clarifies. "It's about power."

"No it isn't," Rose answers.

He shoots Fi in the back of the head, splattering blood onto Rose. "It's always about power."

Rose looks the man in the eyes, the anger, the hate. She knows this is a dream, it's her dream. She can control her dream. She leaps at him and grabs hold of the collar of his shirt to lift his head up and punches him with the other. Over and over again. When there's nothing left to recognize him.

"You think you scare me? This is my dream! I have all the power here!" Rose yells.

"I told you just to shoot him," Fi says, smiling.

Once she gains control over the nightmare, it ends.

Lucious

There's a lot of shouting. It's faint, probably outside. "I'll deal with that later. If it's such a problem they would've knocked on my door or they'll talk to Fi about it," Rose says to herself as the shouting gets closer. Then there's a knock at her door. "Oh great. Now it's my problem," she says, rolling out of bed. Her mind still feels hungover on the fear and loss of her nightmares. She limps to her door, still sore from carrying Fi home.

She opens the door to be face to face with the man that almost killed Fi.

"Morning, my lady," he says sarcastically.

Rose's eyes go wide, this must be a dream. *There's no way he found my home.*

"I see you're a woman of few words. I can respect that. Your friend was quite the opposite, you must be the level head one, it's a pleasure to meet you," he says, holding out his hand.

Rose continues to stare, thinking this can't be real.

"I'm Lucious," he says, still holding out his hand. "And you are?" He finally says, after an awkward moment.

"Dreaming," she says, and closes the door.

"Ouch. Haven't been met like that before," Lucious says, opening the door. "Is that the hospitality I heard so much about your family?"

It's at this moment when Rose realizes she is awake, "What do you want?" She says, staring.

"I see you just woke up, so I'll allow that disrespect this time," he says, holding his hand out again. "I'm Lucious."

"Rose," she says, looking at his open hand.

"Not a shaker?" He asks.

"I'm a hugger," she says sarcastically.

"I don't know about that," he says.

"What are you doing in my home?" Rose asks.

"I'm here for you," he says back, startling Rose.

"What about me?" She says, sizing him up and glaring into his eyes.

"Here to talk, don't worry. Nothing malicious."

"Talk about what?" Rose asks defensively.

"What happened yesterday. You could have killed me, but you didn't. Even when your boyfriend begged you to," Lucious says.

"What about it?" Rose asks.

"You have honor. I respect that," he says.

"You followed a girl home to tell her you respect her?" Rose asks. "Boy you sure know how to treat a lady."

"I didn't follow you personally," he says with a grin. "Remember your friend used me as a punching bag. Though, I did beat him like a sack of potatoes, so I guess we're even," he says with a chuckle.

"Your point?" Rose asks, even more upset.

"Neither of us were in any condition to walk on our own. I am told you were pretty easy to follow. Did you even think to check for any tails? Sloppy," he says.

Rose's eyes widened in fear, "where is Fi?!" She demands.

"Who's Fi?" Lucious says, looking confused.

"The one that nearly killed you last night," Rose says confidently with a side of fear for Fi.

"Ah, that's his name. When I visited him he was very angry. Something about 'next time I see you I said I was going to kill you', then he tried to stand. It was a hilarious act. You should've seen him try to stand. I made sure to bust a leg when we fought. Just to, you know, raise the stakes," Lucious says, almost laughing.

Rose reaches to her hip to feel an empty holster, then looks at Lucious with violent intent.

"Hey now, I wouldn't let myself into your home to kill someone, your friend is fine. Healing a little slowly, but he's fine."

"Raise the stakes?" Rose asks, repeating a line Lucious said for him to elaborate on.

"You know, bust a leg so they can't run off, makes them fight harder. Triggers the 'to the death' thought process," he says.

"How is crippling someone in a fight honorable?" Rose says.

"They fight to the death from that. Cripple a leg and they don't beg for mercy. They know what's at stake. They die with honor," he says.

"You have a messed up sense of honor," Rose says, visibly disgusted with him.

"Well, here we are still standing. Well, not your friend, he may need a few days off his feet," he says, taunting her.

"Wait, how are you up and about after that fight?" Rose asks.

"Now you're asking the right questions. I just have better doctors," he says cryptically.

"You shouldn't even be walking after that fight," Rose says.

"Like I said, better doctors," he says, grinning.

"If all you want is to mock me, you may go. Don't let the gate hit you on your way out," Rose says, annoyed.

"Oh I like you," Lucious says.

"I don't like you. So if we're done, you can go," she says.

"But my lady, we aren't done," he says in a mocking tone. "We need to talk about your armaments. I know you've been trying to build alliances, I know what kind of firepower you have. You pose a big threat to everything I'm building," he says.

Rose crosses her arms and glares at him, "you're not taking my weapons or my people," she says. "I know what you do with other settlements."

"That could be a problem. There is a solution though. Join us. My manpower, your weapons, no one could oppose us. We're rebuilding civilization," he says.

"No one to oppose us? You mean killing everyone that doesn't conform?" Rose asks.

"Humans fear change, no doubt some won't support society going back to the way it was. Someone would have to organize everything," he says.

"A dictator," Rose says. "Yeah, not interested."

"With this much firepower, if you're not with me, you're a threat to me. Think about what you're doing," he says, trying to intimidate her. "You seem to know what happens when people are a threat to me."

"I know fear, you don't scare me," she says.

"You don't know me yet," he says.

"I've looked fear in the eyes without flinching. You're nothing," she says, trying to intimidate him back.

"You must be talking about Rand," Lucious says. The name startles Rose. "Yeah, I heard all about him too. His story is legendary. Standing up for what he knew to be right, even killing his very parents as the story goes."

"You don't know my brother," Rose says, defensively.

"You're right about that, I never knew him personally, but the stories of his bravery go everywhere. And yours," he says, bringing the topic back to Rose, "you killed him. You did what you knew to be right and killed him in cold blood. I mean, damn!" He shouts. "With conviction like that, you are a massive threat to anyone that opposes you. And when it comes to something as big as rebuilding, I can't afford any threats. I'm sure you understand."

"You admire me for sticking to what's right then try to coerce me into joining you which goes against everything i believe in?" Rose asks.

"You're just as sharp as they say. I really like you," Lucious says.

"I'm not joining you," she says sternly.

"Rand would," he says suddenly. His audacity shocks Rose. "Well, if he were still alive, he would," he finishes.

"My brother would've put a bullet in your skull once you trespassed in my home," Rose says offensively.

"Those aren't the stories I've been told. But I'm sure you knew him better," Lucious says, taunting Rose.

Rose glares into his eyes, "I know my brother better than anyone. Better than any story. How did you even hear of my brother? I don't recognize you at all."

"Your scouts are very good storytellers," Lucious says. "They tell dramatic stories very well. I see why your morale is so high."

"My people are telling everyone that?" Rose asks.

"It's definitely inspiring. You just have to be more careful with who you tell the location of your home to," Lucious says grinning.

"So did you follow us or did you hear from my people?" Rose asks, confused.

"I heard your home base from your scouts, in fact, we were watching you the other night. I was planning a meet and greet myself soon, but your friend definitely caught me off guard and kicked the hell out of me. I had people follow you to know who I should visit next. So this trip was inevitable," he says.

"If I kick you out now will you choose violence?" Rose asks, tired of dealing with him.

"If you kick me out without working a peace deal, it will lead to violence," he says.

"I'm not working for you," Rose says.

"I hope you change your mind. Conflict... is gonna happen. Sooner or later, we will meet again. Until then, farewell. It was a pleasure meeting you," Lucious nods towards Rose, then signals his people to leave with him.

Rose quickly turns around and finally sees her pistol on her bed. Must've fallen out of her holster when she slept. She grabs it and runs back out to catch up to Lucious, acting as a sort of armed escort out.

She finally catches up behind Lucious in the courtyard. She looks to her left and sees Fi leaning against someone walking out of the infirmary. Once he sees Rose, he makes eye contact and nods. Rose walks over to them watching Lucious's people continue to the gate. All of her people are out watching Lucious and his armed men.

Lucious turns to see Fi, then follows his gaze to Rose behind. "Oh, you even see your guests out, I'm flattered," he says.

Fi turns to Lucious, glares at him for a moment, then turns his attention back to Rose.

Rose just ignores Lucious.

"Anyway, Fi, it was a pleasure talking with you. Next time, I agree, it will be to the death," Lucious says with laughter.

Rose gets up next to Fi and they both watch in silence as Lucious leaves. "The audacity of that bitch," Rose says, once they're gone.

The sudden line makes Fi burst into laughter.

"Are you alright?" She asks, trying not to laugh.

"Oww," he says, clenching his ribs. "Banged up but I'll live," he says, with pain ending his laughter. Upon seeing Rose, the man helping Fi sets him up on his own and returns inside. All the guards get up on the wall to watch Lucious leave.

Rose hugs Fi tight, her arms wrapping around the bottom of his ribs. "I'm so glad you're alright."

"Again, ow," Fi says, "But I'm glad you're here."

"How did he get in?" Rose asks, concerned.

"He showed up with an army and said he would be peaceful as long as he could talk to you. Everyone was afraid. The guards eventually let him in and someone squealed where your room was," Fi says.

"What did he say to you?" Rose asks.

"Nothing important. I didn't give him anything," Fi says.

"So how big was his army?" Rose asks cautiously.

"Filip said it was at least twice the size of what we have here," Fi looks concerned at Rose, "we need more people. The odds are greatly stacked against us."

"I agree," Rose says. "He's gone, but he may still be watching. Let's not do anything that can be seen from outside the walls for a bit."

"So what did big, tall, and malicious want?" Fi asks, referring to Lucious.

"He said he's rebuilding society and he wants to rule like a dictator," Rose starts.

"Not sure about the -tator part, but he's definitely a dick," Fi jokes. They both laugh, causing Fi more pain. "I didn't get to thank you for carrying me back here," he says, changing the topic.

"You were mostly unconscious, it's fine," Rose says.

"I guess we're even now," Fi says.

"I guess so," Rose says back with a smile.

"I hope you didn't give him what he wanted this time too," Fi says, destroying Rose's smile.

"I didn't give him anything. He threatened war. We need to be more cautious and strengthen our defenses," Rose says.

"You should've ended this yesterday. When I beat him down. You had an easy shot," Fi says, running the mood.

"You would've died! I would've too. They had us outnumbered and outgunned. I made the best decision I could there," Rose says.

"You had a shot before they came in. We were alone," Fi says.

"I'm done talking about this," Rose says, glaring at him.

"You're not the one that nearly died fighting him just for his life to be spared," Fi says angrily. "You don't want to talk about this, well I don't want him breathing."

"Enough. I'm not losing you too. Now drop it," Rose says.

"Fine. Next move?" Fi asks, still angry.

"Work on our defenses and get more soldiers. I presume you want to take over the defense planning?" Rose asks.

"Yeah, I'll do that. I'll talk to Oscar about further scouting," Fi says, finally pushing past that anger.

"Thank you. I have other things to do," she says, walking away towards her quarters. *Sparing Lucious was the best move. I'm sure you'll understand eventually,* Rose thinks to herself.

What Comes Next

Rose makes it to her room and grabs her sword and begins swinging it. The broken sword is more her size, lighter, and faster. Working on the footwork and the muscles for a fight. She's getting better, she can now swing her sword pretty fast. She practices the movements her father tried to teach her, and the movements her brother did teach her.

After an exhausting sword workout, Rose heads down to the guard shack by the wall to pick up ammo for her pistol and her rifle she leaves there. "I'm heading to the range, open the gate please," she calls to Filip.

"Right away, my lady," he replies, opening the gate.

She heads out to the range and is glad to see it's empty. She sets up a new target and moves Back to the firing line about one hundred feet away. She loads up her rifle and takes aim. First three shots hit the edges of the board. Next three shots hit around the edge again. Low and to the right. *How did Fi say to fix this?* She thinks. She aims up and to the left of the bullseye and shoots again. Those shots landed on the right side of the board, so far from a bullseye. *What am I doing wrong?* She shoots until she hears the click of the bolt, empty. She sets the rifle down and draws her pistol. Three shots. One hits the bullseye, the other to the top right corner, and the bottom right corner. She doesn't understand what's wrong with her form. She fires the remainder of her mag with a few bullseyes.

Suddenly Rose feels like she's being watched. She quickly turns, her back facing the wall, her right hand still on the table with her empty guns. She scans her surroundings intently, looking for anything that could be looking back. She's confident she didn't see anything, but still feels off, she turns slightly to the table and quickly starts loading a mag for her pistol. Then some leaves rustle, causing her to panic and jump to the direction of the sound. *That's enough,* she thinks, slamming the partially loaded mag into the pistol then chambering a round.

"That's enough," she calls out, "Come out now."

There's just silence.

The silence makes it worse. Who or what is so much worse when you can't see it. It could be anything, or anyone. She just grabs her rifle and the empty mag, then takes off running to the gate. She rounds the corner to the front gate and calls out for help.

The gate opens and several soldiers come out with guns just as Rose makes it to the gate.

"What is it?" Oscar asks.

"Something was watching me from the trees," Rose says.

"We're on it," Oscar says, leading a handful of troops out to the makeshift range.

Rose takes a moment to breath, then finishes loading her pistol mag from the guard shack. She leaves her rifle there, then goes back out to the range. She stands where she was when she felt whatever something was watching her. She looks out through the trees to see her people moving around out there.

"If it was a wild animal this noise would definitely scare it away," she says to herself. She grabs the ammo she left and heads back inside.

Rose visits Fi in the infirmary. "How are you feeling?" She asks as she enters.

"Hey Rose, sorry about earlier. I'm in a lot of pain," Fi says.

"I understand," Rose says, grabbing his hand.

"I've just been in constant fight or flight since that fight," Fi says.

"I know, I've been through this before," Rose says back.

"Right, Rand. This isn't like that," Fi says.

"Yeah, you're breathing," she says.

There's a moment of silence between them, "Doctor said I'll be on my feet in a few days. I'll be out there scouting," Fi says.

"Are we going to fight?" Rose asks cautiously.

"What kind of question is that? Of course he needs to die," Fi says.

"But at what cost? I want to try to negotiate with him. Try to find peace before anyone dies," Rose says.

"Peace? Are you forgetting about the people he's murdered?!" Fi says, raising his voice.

"I can stop the killing. I'm sure of it," Rose says.

"He dies!" Fi shouts, then flinching in pain.

"Everyone will die!" Rose yells back. "Everyone I care about is here," Rose starts, calmly, "Everyone is safe in our walls. If we start a war we risk everything. I'm not about to watch everyone I care about die again. I'm not losing my home, again."

Fi looks in her eyes, "If we do this smart only he will die," Fi says.

"How?" Rose asks, frustrated he can't give up his pride.

"When I'm healed, I will hunt him and kill him myself. No one will know," he says.

"Assassinate?" Rose asks.

"Yes, no one will know," he says.

"And how would you get that close without anyone knowing?" Rose asks.

"I'll stalk him awhile, find his patrols, his routines. I will find an opening and take him," Fi says with much determination.

"And you will do this knowing full well that it just might set his people on a rampage?" Rose asks.

Fi sighs and breaks eye contact. "He doesn't deserve to live," he says. "With all the lives he's taken, he can't live. He'll just take more." Fi looks into Rose's eyes again, "this isn't about me, this about all those people he killed and all the people he will kill."

"So this has nothing to do with pride?" She asks, finally understanding.

"Nothing to do with pride. This is for them," Fi says.

"You sound like my brother," Rose says.

"Your brother was a great man. He could make the hard choices," Fi says.

Rose sighs. "Let me try negotiating first. If I can stop the bloodshed we can save the people he hasn't killed yet. Save who we care about."

"And if that fails, or if he kills again, I'll kill him myself," Fi says.

"Okay," Rose says. "Okay."

"So, what are you going to do until then?" Fi asks.

"I'm going to visit my brother's grave," Rose says.

"Oh," Fi says. "Say hi for me."

Rose smiles, "get well soon," she says, letting go of his hand starting to leave the infirmary.

"Don't go alone," Fi calls out.

"I'll take Oscar," Rose says, turning back around.

"Oscar?" Fi asks.

"My brother trusted him to lead. I'll be fine," Rose says, smiling back.

"Be safe," Fi says.

"I will," Rose says, leaving the infirmary.

Rose walks out to the courtyard looking for Oscar. Not seeing him, she heads to the gate.

"My lady," Filip says, seeing her approach.

"Eyo, Filip," Rose says.

"Tell me you're not going out there alone this time."

"I'm not, I'm looking for Oscar. Have you seen him?" She asks.

"Oscar, yeah, I just saw him. After searching the woods he went to the mess hall," Filip says.

"Great, thanks," Rose says, heading towards the mess hall.

Rose gets to the mess hall just in time to bump into Oscar leaving.

"Oscar," Rose greets.

"Yes, my lady?" Oscar responds, changing his direction to her.

"Would you like to accompany me as I go speak to my brother?" Rose asks.

"That's an odd request," Oscar says, expecting it to be a joke. "But if you need my talents, I'll go."

"Great," Rose says, smiling. "I want to talk to my brother again. Get some advice about this."

"Am I missing something?" Oscar asks, thinking now this is a joke being played at his expense.

"What do you mean?" Rose asks curiously.

Seeing the sincerity in her eyes Oscar doesn't know how to proceed. He finally asks, "isn't your brother… dead?"

"Yeah," she says slowly, not sure where he's going with it.

"If he's dead, where are we going?" Oscar asks.

"To the place he's buried," Rose says, raising an eyebrow. "I would like to talk to him."

Oscar finally understands, "oh, of course my lady. Lead the way."

"You got everything you need for this trip?" Rose asks.

"Yup. Just had a snack too," Oscar says.

"Oh yeah, I should probably get some food before we head out," Rose says.

"I got you," Oscar says, reaching into a small pouch hanging from his belt and pulling out an apple. "Here," he says, handing it to her.

"Oh thanks," she says, accepting the fruit. "Nice snack pouch."

"Snack pouch, nice one," Oscar chuckles.

"Alright, let's head out," Rose says, walking to the gate with Oscar at her side.

"Be safe my lady, you too Oscar," Filip says, closing the gate behind them.

Meeting of Grave Importance

"If you don't mind me asking, Rose, what was Rand like before everything happened?" Oscar asks.

"He was everything an older brother should be," she says smiling. "His best attributes became stronger when the machines attacked."

"Was he always so," Oscar looks for the right word, "... determined on doing things his way?"

"That was an attribute that was brought out when everything happened," Rose says. "For the better and the worse."

"The better?" Oscar asks.

"He was very strategic, once he made a plan, that was it. There was no changing it. It helped with time sensitive problems, but hindered overall preparations as he wouldn't let anyone else make suggestions," Rose says.

"Yeah, I remember that," Oscar says with a chuckle. "Was he always so brave?"

"He would always stand up for me and what he believed in," Rose says, her smile growing. "If anyone tried anything, he would stop them. He had a way with people."

"That protectiveness was brought out even more for you," Oscar adds.

"It was, yeah," Rose says proudly. "Until he killed for me," saying that killed her smile.

"Yeah I remember that too," Oscar says. "What about him in combat? He killed Havoc and Helen, how great was he?"

"He was great with one on one, the more you add the more he struggled," Rose says.

"But it was enough to kill Havoc," Oscar adds.

"I didn't see the fight, he didn't tell me how he won. I can only assume all the training my father gave him was enough to overthrow him," Rose says.

"Did your father train him himself?" Oscar asks.

"Our parents were very busy, when they weren't they would train us, but for the most part we were trained by some soldiers that were trained by my father," Rose says.

"We?" Oscar asks.

"Yeah, I wasn't much of a fighter before, but they did try to teach me," Rose says.

"You're a fighter like Rand?" Oscar asks.

"No, well not yet I guess," Rose says back.

"Didn't teach you or didn't learn?" Oscar asks.

"I didn't want to be a fighter. I hate killing, but recent events have had me practicing," she says.

"Is Fi training you?" Oscar asks.

"Fi doesn't use swords, I'm just going through what my brother taught me," Rose says.

"Would you like to spar sometime?" Oscar asks. "I want to see you in action."

"I don't know, I'm not a fighter yet. Plus we're both really busy," Rose says, making excuses.

"We can make time. Training alone is good for the basics, but without a live opponent you're really not learning anything," Oscar says.

"True," Rose says, "I'm worried about how it would look."

"It would look awesome," Oscar says excitedly.

"I mean, I'm not a fighter, you would beat me. How would that look to everyone else? The leader getting beat by the scout," Rose says.

"You care too much about your image. Our people know you're not a fighter, you're the heart. I think seeing you train publicly will keep morale high. Everyone already looks up to you as our leader, but as a warrior? More respect," Oscar says.

"Thanks," Rose says, smiling.

"So what did you do before everything went to hell?" Oscar asks.

"I'm fifteen, so nothing really," Rose says.

"You're fifteen?" Oscar says in disbelief.

"Yeah," Rose says nervously.

"Damn, you're the most strategic-thinking person I know, and you are fifteen?" Oscar says.

"Halfway to sixteen, I think. Haven't been keeping track of days since everything went to hell," Rose says.

"Wow, was Rand eighteen? He definitely acted like an adult," Oscar says.

"He's about three years older," Rose says.

"So eighteen," Oscar says.

"Practically eighteen, but not quite," Rose says.

"Wow you two grew up fast," Oscar says.

"This is going to blow your mind, but Fi is only seventeen too," Rose says.

"Really? Is anyone here an adult?" Oscar asks.

"Everyone but your great leaders are," Rose says, smirking.

"Wow, even more respect to you," Oscar says.

"So what did you do before?" Rose asks.

"I was a messenger," Oscar says. "I love running."

"That's why my brother appointed you as the head scout," Rose says.

"Well, the day everything went to hell, Havoc visited our town. He spoke of a powerful adversary that he needed more fighters to defeat," Oscar says.

"So my father was trying to fight, he didn't just join them," Rose says, happily.

"No, the next day the machines attacked. Havoc was there, they killed everyone that wouldn't work with them. I wasn't a fighter, I was a delivery boy. I joined to be spared. He had us collect all the bodies," Oscar says, all emotion drained from his voice, "I carried my family, one at a time to the collection wagon," Oscar had a hard time speaking. "Anyways, after joining we found out what happened with the soldiers he brought out, it was an ambush."

"No," Rose says in shock.

"Yes, Havoc led them out and executed them so no one would be able to fight back against the machines," Oscar says, looking away.

"I'm so sorry," Rose says.

"After Rand defeated him, we were glad that man was dead, but scared of what Rand would do," Oscar says.

"Then he started killing those that surrendered," Rose says.

"Yeah. Though, at that point I'm sure most of them were waiting for the release of death," Oscar says.

"That's why you follow Fi and I, we stopped Havoc, and aren't violent like my brother," Rose says.

"Exactly. Okay, no more sad stuff," Oscar says, clearing his throat and forcing a smile.

"Tell me more about your city," Rose says, "If you want of course."

"Of course," Oscar starts.

They continue talking about how things were for both of them before the machines attacked.

Rose and Oscar arrive at the location where Rand was buried.

"Can you give me a moment?" Rose asks, as they round the corner of the massive building in front of the graveyard.

"Sure, my lady," Oscar says. "I'll be here, watching your back," he says, leaning against the building.

"Thanks," Rose says, looking him in the eyes, then going to the graves. She slows down to honor each grave she passes, looking at the head stone. Finally she looks past to see a figure by where Rand was buried. She approaches, "Oscar can I get a moment with my brother?" She asks.

"Of course," the man says, getting to his feet. The voice was not Oscar. "I'm not Oscar, but who am I to stop you from your family reunion?" Lucious says.

Upon hearing his voice again, Rose panics and draws her pistol, keeping it at a low ready. The surprise on her face tells Lucious all he needs to know.

"I didn't expect to see you here either," he says. "You should really put that thing away," looking at her gun.

"What are you doing here?" Rose asks.

"Just came by to speak to someone," Lucious says.

"You knew I'd be here," she mumbles to herself.

Lucious looks her in the eyes with a teasing look. He's playing mind games now.

"How did you know I'd be here now?" Rose asks, raising her voice and gun a little.

"I don't know what you're talking about," Lucious says, with a knowing grin. "I just came here for a chat."

Rose is even more panicked now, he's in her head.

"Why don't you lower your gun," Lucious says calmly. "You wouldn't want anyone to get hurt, would you?"

Rose is panicked, but keeps her composure. No shaking, no outward fear. Only her eyes show emotion.

"You really shouldn't be outside your walls alone," Lucious says hauntingly.

"I-I'm not alone," she says, trying to shake the fear. *I'm not alone.*

Lucious looks past her then says, "well not this time. I see you're learning. But one guy isn't much, aren't you their leader?"

Rose hears commotion behind her, she looks over her shoulder to see Oscar with his hands on his head and three armed men behind him. Her heart races.

"Isn't she your leader?" Lucious calls out to Oscar.

"Screw you," Oscar says back, immediately getting thrown to the ground.

Rose disengages the safety on her pistol, "let him go!" She demands, pointing her pistol at the men.

The three men point their rifles at her.

"That's not a smart move," Lucious says.

"Shoot him," Oscar says, his face in the dirt.

"That would be the worst decision you could possibly make," Lucious says back. "There's four of us. What happens when you fire a shot?"

"Shoot him! We may die, but Fi can still lead," Oscar shouts.

Rose turns to Lucious, pointing her pistol at his head, "let him go," she demands again. Hearing Fi's name while looking at Lucious reminds her of her nightmare.

"Are you really going to sacrifice yourself and him?" Lucious asks.

Oscar, seeing Rose conflicted, says, "it's a sacrifice I'm willing to make," he springs into action, just to get kicked right back down.

"Oscar!" Rose calls out, sliding her finger to the trigger.

"Look out guys, we've got a badass over here," Lucious says, mocking Oscar.

"Go to hell," Oscar says.

"Is that where you want our next reunion to be? I can arrange that," Lucious says, smugly. "As for you," he says, looking at Rose. "I really like you, so I'll give you one last warning. Put the gun down. I didn't come here to kill anyone."

Rose finally lowers her gun, "I didn't come here to kill either. Just wanted to visit my brother," she says.

"Then holster that bad boy and come over here," Lucious says, gesturing for her to get next to him by Rand's grave. "Don't worry about them," he says, giving a hand signal to his men as they lower their guns.

Rose kneels down by Rand's grave, next to Lucious.

"Tell me, how was Rand before everything went to hell?" Lucious asks.

Rose pauses, takes a moment to think, then remembers the person her brother was before everything happened making her sad. But in remembering how he was and how he changed, she remembers how she was and how she changed. Pride for herself, pride for the woman she's becoming over powers that sadness and fills her with confidence. *This is how I'll make peace. Once I set my mind to something, there's nothing I can't do,* she thinks to herself. She lets out a sigh, "he was always brave. A great fighter, he could beat anyone one on one. And his conviction was unshakable."

"All amazing traits for a leader," Lucious compliments. "I see those same traits in you," he says, catching her off guard.

"I'm nothing like my brother," Rose says, rejecting the compliment.

"Well, I'm not sure how you are in combat, but I've seen your courage first hand. And the story of you offing your brother, now that's conviction," Lucious says. "You and your brother are fighters at heart."

"So you know my brother killed our parents when they told us to kneel," Rose starts.

"Conviction," Lucious responds with a nod.

"So you know I won't bend the knee to you," there's a pause between the two, "I know there's a way we can work this out peacefully. No bloodshed, no kneeling," Rose says.

"Now that's how you negotiate," Lucious says, "No threats, you just say how it is. Okay, let's see if we can work something out."

"Good, first term, no more killing," Rose says.

"I hate killing, but sometimes it needs to be done," Lucious says.

"You don't need to kill," Rose says. "No one needs to die."

"What of your brother?" Lucious says immediately, almost as if he knew what she would say.

"That's different," Rose says, trying to justify it in her head.

"There are two kinds of people. Those that say no killing, but kill, and those that hate killing but kill when it's needed," Lucious says, calling her out.

"How many lives have you taken?" Rose asks angrily.

"Personally or," Lucious says, intentionally angering her more.

"You can't even count how many, can you?" Rose says, getting more angry. "I've killed one because he was a threat to everyone else."

"I only kill when they're a threat to others," Lucious says. "You just lived a sheltered life."

"Ha, you think I've been sheltered? Everything in my life has been a challenge," Rose states.

"A personal challenge, or something the world threw at you to end you?" Lucious asks.

"Everything I've endured was -," Rose gets interrupted.

"Rand fixing your problems by killing," Lucious interjects. "Your brother and I are very similar, I just wish you were more like him."

Rose is speechless.

"You hold yourself up high telling people you don't kill, while letting those around you kill for you. I acknowledge it when I need to kill. We are not the same," Lucious says.

"I'm not a killer!" Rose says back.

"Of course not, your friends do that for you," Lucious says.

"You executed an entire town!" Rose shouts.

"So did you," Lucious calmly replies.

Rose's eyes widen, *how does he know about that?* She thinks.

"Oh was I not supposed to know about that?" Lucious teases. "I've been watching you before we ever met."

"You were watching me outside my home," Rose says.

"I'm told you're a good shot," Lucious says with a smirk.

"How long have you been watching us?" Rose asks.

"Long enough," Lucious responds cryptically.

"Long enough for what?" Rose asks.

"Long enough to find your weakness, your base's weakness, and all your strengths," Lucious says. "Looks like the negotiations are in my turf."

Rose is in shock, what can she say to that?

"I'll let you process that for a moment," Lucious says, seeing her in shock. "I wasn't going to attack without saying hello first. I just needed to know everything in case I had to shoot my way out - or in."

Rose is afraid now, not for herself, but for her people. For Fi. "Limit killing to only absolutely necessary," Rose says.

"There you go," Lucious says. "My term is you join us. In alliance or at my capitol."

"I'm not leaving my home," Rose protests.

"Then join us in alliance. We're rebuilding society. Like I said before, I can't have someone as powerful as you with weapons like that against me," Lucious says.

"Fi would never agree to an alliance with you," Rose says.

"Fi's not here, you are," Lucious says.

"I don't want an alliance with you either," she says.

"Either that, or give up your big guns," Lucious says.

Rose thinks for a moment and sighs, "What would this alliance look like?"

"Asking the right questions. We'll set up a trade network, we give you what you need, you give us what we need, as well as tribute," Lucious says.

"Tribute?" Rose questions.

"Yes, I will have law and order, with that comes tribute. Those that live underneath will be protected, and they will pay for the added benefits," he says.

"First thing you're setting up is taxes?" Rose snarks.

"The payment will be spread around so everyone gets stronger together," Lucious says.

"Isn't that what the trade is for?" Rose asks. "Sounds like you just want more for yourself."

"Of course I want more, if everyone under me was as powerful as me everyone would be fighting for power," Lucious says.

"So this tribute is to keep everyone else weaker and dependent on you," Rose says.

"That's how society works. If everyone had equal power, no one would follow anyone. There would be a lot more violence. You need someone above everyone to give them orders. You need everyone depended on you," Lucious says.

"I will not be part of that," Rose says sternly. "Trade routes yes, less killing, yes, but I won't be a part of that. Everyone should be self-sufficient."

"If everyone was on equal ground everyone would try to lead their own way. No one would follow, that leads to chaos," Lucious says.

"Respect will get others to follow. You've watched my home and my people, so you've seen what they're capable of. And yet, they follow me. I'm smaller than most of them, I'm weaker than most of them, but they follow me with respect because I treat them with respect back," Rose says.

"We'll see how long that lasts. Fear controls people better. Rand had absolute control over everyone, you have some control over your people. Fi keeps the others in line," Lucious mocks.

"I guess you haven't spied on us enough then," Rose says, standing up.

"Are you going to join me?" Lucious says, standing up with her.

"Not with those terms. If you consider us a threat, you better come up with a compromise," Rose says aggressively.

"Damn, you're outnumbered here and you still threaten me," Lucious says loudly. "This is why I like you. You are fearless."

Rose looks him in the eyes, "I'm done playing your games," and turns to walk away.

"If anyone else said those words to me it would be their last. Rose," he says, laying his hand on her shoulder to turn her around.

"Don't touch me!" Rose shouts, throwing him to the ground.

"Now I'm impressed," Lucious says, getting up. "I just threatened you and you swept me off my feet."

"I've said my piece, if you want peace you need to make some compromises," Rose says, walking to Oscar.

"I'll take it under consideration. You're just going to walk away?" Lucious asks.

"Gonna stop me?" Rose says, not even turning to face him, walking off with Oscar.

Lucious smiles, "you came here to talk to your brother," he says, gesturing to the tombstone.

Rose stops in her tracks and sighs. She throws a glance over her shoulder at Lucious that startles him.

"I'm all talked out, I'll see you again to renegotiate our terms," Lucious says, gathering his people and heading out, opposite the way Rose is.

Rose and Oscar watch them leave, as soon as they're out of sight Rose says, "okay. Now I can finally have peace with my brother," and walks back to the tombstone.

"I'm not taking you out of my sight this time, my lady," Oscar says.

"You can be close, just stay out of earshot. I want some privacy with my brother," she says, not even looking at Oscar.

"Hello brother," Rose starts, getting on her knees. "It's been awhile. I wanted this visit to be about how we're doing and how great everything is, but after that incident with Lucious, I'm just full of anger. The worst part is, he's right. And I want to kill him. But I know I shouldn't. If you were here he'd already be dead," she says with a chuckle. "And there lies the problem. But if I condone killing, then where does the line get drawn?"

"The line is drawn where you need to draw it," Rose imagines Rand saying.

"You always told me to not take a life, I don't know if I can," Rose says.

"Never take a life out of emotion," Rose imagines Rand's voice again.

"I don't want to become a killer," Rose says.

"Then don't. One man to save everyone you care about isn't bad," Rose imagines Rand saying.

"That leads you down a path of death and destruction. I won't go down that road," Rose says.

"Then let Fi kill him," Rose imagines him saying.

"That makes him right. Lucious can't be right," Rose says. "This didn't help like I thought it would. Goodbye brother," she says, standing up.

Oscar notices Rose standing and begins walking towards her. "Get everything you were looking for?" He asks, with his rifle in hand.

"No. I got more of what I didn't want," Rose responds. "Let's get home, quickly."

On the walk home Oscar asks, "how would Rand deal with Lucious?"

"Upon finding him beating up Fi, he would've shot him there and then," Rose says.

"If he spared him then, how would he deal with Lucious when he came to our home?" Oscar asks.

"He would've shot him in the head the moment he caught him trespassing," Rose says.

"Trying to bring peace is noble, and standing out from your brother like that is great, but at what cost?" Oscar asks.

Rose is lost in thoughts. Trying desperately to convince herself this is the right move.

"Rose?" Oscar says, trying to get her attention.

"I don't want to talk right now," she says. "Let's just get home."

They have a long silent walk home.

We're With You

Rose notices a lot more guards on the wall around their base.

"Rose is here!" Filip shouts as he opens the gate.

Fi is the first one out of the base, limp running to Rose, "You're okay!" Fi says, grabbing her tightly in a hug. Other soldiers follow after, surrounding them.

"Of course I'm okay," Rose says confused, "Why wouldn't I be?" She asks.

"Lucious stopped by, told us he ran into you and you threatened him," Fi says, releasing Rose. "We feared the worst."

"I'm fine," Rose says.

"Did he hurt you?" Fi asks.

"I hurt him," Rose responds. "He wants us to join him."

"I hope you told him no," Fi says, looking concerned.

"That's when I hurt him," Rose says.

"Let's talk about this inside," Fi says, leaning against Rose and gesturing to go ahead.

"This can't be a decision between just you and me," Rose says, "Bring everyone not on guard to the command room."

"I really hope you aren't considering his offer," Fi says. "Everyone not guarding the perimeter come to the command room," he shouts.

"We started negotiating, the terms should be decided with all of us," Rose says.

Rose and Fi stand in front of the map table in front of everyone in the command center. Fi is standing beside Rose leaning against the table.

"I went to talk to my brother at his grave and ran into Lucious there. He was the one watching me outside of our walls. He already knew I was going there before I got there. He has spies everywhere," Rose starts.

"Now that's concerning," Fi says. "Did he let on to who it may be?"

"No. I don't want war or death. We started to negotiate. He wants to kill. I told him no killing, he said sometimes people just have to die," Rose says.

"Sometimes, yeah," Fi agrees.

"I got him to only kill when absolutely necessary," Rose says. "Next term is for us to join him. Either in an alliance or in his base. He wants tributes if we stay here."

"Tribute?" Fi asks.

"His plan is to keep everyone else beneath him so no one is powerful enough to overthrow him," Rose says. "Tribute to steal the resources from others, making him stronger while everyone else gets weaker and dependent."

"That scum," Fi says, clenching his fists. "Do I even want to know the if we join their base part?"

"He will disarm us and we'll basically be slaves under him," Rose says.

"Both sound like slavery to me," Fi says.

"I told him my terms and told him we will not kneel. He's going to come up with compromises, I want to make sure everyone here is on board with my decision," Rose says.

"You're our leader, you and Fi," Oscar starts, "we will follow your lead."

"I need to know you guys are all in. This may lead to war, I do not kneel to anyone. I want to make sure everyone here is okay and ready for that," Rose says.

For the first time during a briefing, Fi is taking a backseat. Partly not knowing what to say, and partly just to watch Rose take charge. "Remember, he has a high body count. I still want to kill him," he says.

"You're still injured from your last fight, you're in no shape to fight any time soon," Rose says, looking at his bad leg.

"This man has no honor, he doesn't need a chance. I'll take him out with my rifle," Fi says.

"That would send all of his people into a rage against us. You said the people he showed up here with were more than we have. We don't know how many are in his alliance, where his base is, or how many others are with him," Rose says.

"Unless I take him out at a distance," Fi says. "Find him in the open and take him out without being detected. No one would know."

"You really think you can do that with a leg like that? You still have a bad limp," Rose says.

"My lady, I can be his support," Oscar volunteers. "I can go with him and keep our tracks covered for the shot. Then keep us hidden until we can make it back here."

Rose is quiet, trying to think of a flaw to that plan. Fi smiles with a nod of approval to Oscar. "What if they come straight here, looking for us. They see that two people that want him dead are gone. Nothing we could do to convince them," Rose finally says.

"Tell them it's a scouting run. Two people missing isn't much to go off of," Fi says.

"We could even visit another settlement nearby to establish an alibi," Oscar says.

"You want witnesses to see you were in the area at the time of death?" Rose asks.

Oscar looks bewildered, he didn't think that far yet.

"Sometimes a leap forward requires taking a few steps back," Rose says.

"Sometimes all that's required is the will to jump," Fi says back. "Look, he needs to die. What if he rules his people through fear, if we kill him they may be more peaceful," Fi says. "They may even join us."

"That's a very big if. What if it's the opposite and they go on a murder spree? What if Lucious is the one holding their leash?" Rose says back.

"Those are equally big ifs," Fi responds.

"There will be a massive power vacuum regardless. Who knows how any of them will react," Rose says. "Let's give peace a chance."

"Fine, but one way or another, he will die, eventually," Fi says.

"Eventually," Rose says, agreeing. "But not soon."

"When are you meeting him again?" Fi asks.

"I don't know. Like I said, I told him we won't kneel and he is the one that needs to find the compromise on that," Rose says.

"You said that to his face?" Fi says, surprised.

"Yeah she did, you should've seen her. She really put Lucious in his place," Oscar says.

"Damn, I really did miss a lot," Fi says.

"I was just in a mood," Rose says, trying to deflect.

Everyone around laughs. Rose looks around not understanding why everyone is laughing.

"Putting a man like Lucious in his place because you were in a mood would really make Rand proud," Fi laughs, wrapping his arm around her shoulders.

Rose doesn't know how to respond to that, she does want to be like her brother, but she's unsure if that's how she wants to be like him. She smiles when she feels Fi's arm wrap around her. She places her hand on his, "I'm sure he would be," she says.

"Seems like we don't have anything else to discuss," Fi says. "Not until Lucious comes back with his revised terms."

"So everyone is with me?" Rose asks.

"Everyone is with us," Fi clarifies.

"Everyone is with you," Oscar says. "You two have served us so much, we owe our lives to you two. We have your backs."

Every soldier there shouts back, "I will stand and fight for you Rose and Fi!"

"I will continue to do everything I can to keep us all safe and free," Rose says back.

"As will I," Fi says.

After the cheering ends, Fi says, "we should keep sending out scouts. Maybe we can get enough people to scare Lucious, or in the worst case scenario an army to fight him."

"He has a lot of people, he probably already got everyone nearby under his boot," Rose says.

"My lady, I think it wouldn't hurt for a few scouts at a time," Oscar says.

Rose looks back to Fi for his answer.

Fi looks to Rose, "We need more people. We have the weapons for a fight, but not people."

"The thing is, if something happens, we need everyone here. We can really only spare two. But I don't want just two people going out," Rose says.

"My lady, we were going in teams of two before we knew about Lucious," Oscar says.

"Before we knew about Lucious. Now we know of a much bigger threat out there," Rose says.

"I think it's a good idea. And as long as Lucious isn't at war with us they'll be fine," Fi says to Rose. He looks over to the soldiers, "just don't give Lucious a reason to want to kill you. That's my job."

Oscar smiles, "I can do that," he says.

"I guess it's settled then," Rose says, feeling defeated.

"Hey, don't worry about them," Fi says, gently squeezing her shoulder, "It'll be fine."

"I hope so," Rose says.

"We won't let you down," Oscar says confidently.

"Oscar, I assume you still want to be the main scout?" Fi asks.

"Yes sir," he says. "I got a good partner. I'll rest up and we'll head out in the morning."

"Good," Fi says, looking at Rose, seeing her quiet. "If that's everything, this meeting is adjourned."

Rose nods, "thank you all for your understanding," she says. "We'll meet again when Lucious returns with his terms."

The soldiers leave the building and return to what they were doing.

"That went well," Fi says. "Can you tell me more about your interaction with Lucious?" Fi asks, as everyone leaves.

"That's basically it. He said he's been watching us, he threatened me about not following his terms, I threatened him back about not following my terms, then he left," Rose says.

"When did you hit him?" Fi asks.

"When he threatened me," Rose says. "I turned to leave and he touched me so I threw him."

"He touched you?" Fi says concerned.

"He grabbed my arm as I was walking away, so I threw him to the ground," Rose clarifies.

"Oh nice," Fi says.

145

"He must be all talk, I threw him effortlessly," Rose says, teasing Fi.

"Oh haha," Fi fake laughs. "So what are you going to do now?"

"Exercise," Rose says.

"That was a long walk, both ways, you're still energetic?" Fi asks.

"I got a lot of frustration to get out," Rose says.

"Okay, well it's great you're working hard," Fi says.

Rose begins to move away from Fi, he lightly pulls her back with his arm still on her shoulders, "one more hug before you go."

Rose squishes into his arms. A lot of the frustration leaves with a warming smile. "Thank you."

"No, thank you," Fi says, releasing his arms.

Rose heads to her room and notices the hole in the wall. "Great, forgot about that," she says with a sigh. "Fine, I'll fix it later."

"Alright, let's do this," Rose says, changing into a tank top and shorts to exercise until she falls asleep on the floor.

Calm Day

Rose wakes up on the floor feeling well rested. She yawns and goes to her snack stockpile for some fruit. She looks down at herself, "Right, forgot to change. Minds well," she says, getting back on the floor to exercise. Once she's in good rhythm, there's a knock at the door.

"My lady, you in there?" A muffled voice calls out through the door.

"What is it?" Rose calls out, continuing her push-ups.

"The scouts found something, Fi told me to get you immediately," he says.

Rose moves to a seated position to catch her breath for a moment. "What kind of something?" She calls back.

"A good something, Oscar found people," he says.

"Oh good," Rose says, getting up and moving to the door. She opens the door and the soldier freezes, not expecting to see her like that.

"Um," the soldier says, turning around, "You good?"

Rose is confused, "What you're talking about."

"You're um," he says, still facing away.

"I'm covered," Rose says, looking down at herself. "You can face me."

"Yeah, I mean, okay," he turns back around. He looks very uncomfortable keeping his head up looking directly into her eyes.

"Okay, tell Fi I'll be there in just a minute," Rose says.

"Yes my lady," he says, holding uncomfortable eye contact.

"I feel like you're looking into my soul, please stop," Rose says with a chuckle.

"Sorry my lady," the soldier says, looking at the ground between them.

"Okay, I'm going to change then I'll be there," Rose says, closing the door. She wipes off her forehead and puts on a shirt, pants, and overcoat. Then heads down to the command room, where she expects everyone to be.

"Ah Rose," Fi says, glancing at her as she walks in. "Took you long enough," he says, focusing back on the radio.

"Well I'm here," Rose says. "What's this about?"

"Oscar made contact with a group of people in a pretty large town," Fi says.

"Oh, are they friendly?" Rose asks.

"So far," Fi says. "They're open to an alliance too."

Rose gets excited, "how many people?" She asks.

"Oscar said it's a pretty big town, no accurate count yet," Fi says. "Waiting on Oscar, he's trying to talk them into negotiations with us."

"And when he does, we're going," Rose says, referring to herself and Fi.

"There's no one I'd like more to be with me during these negotiations," Fi says.

Rose smiles and waits patiently.

Suddenly the radio springs to life with voices, "They're willing to negotiate, when should they expect us?"

Fi looks at Rose, "first thing in the morning?" He asks.

Rose looks back and nods, "sounds great."

"Home base to scout team, first thing in the morning," Fi says.

"Affirm, first thing in the morning," the radio man repeats back.

"That went well," Fi says, turning his attention to the troops around him. "Sounds like we're going to be making some new friends, I need everyone to be presentable. If you're not guarding or scouting, I need you strengthening yourself or the team. Major focus on team drills. Go," Fi says, as all the troops leave.

"So who's out there?" Rose asks.

"Didn't get a name. Scouts reported they aren't too trusting yet, which is why we're going to keep it at just two when we go to negotiate," Fi says.

"I meant the scouts," Rose says.

"Oh, Oscar and Damian," Fi says.

"Oscar has done a lot for us. I don't recognize Damian though," Rose says.

"He's one of the scouts. He was with us when we attacked Aida," Fi says.

"Oh, I'm just not good with names then," Rose says.

"I feel you. It's like there's only four soldiers here that stand out," Fi says.

"The rest just blend into the crowd," Rose says in agreement.

"Well, we are better trained and better leaders," Fi says with a smirk.

"That is true," Rose says with a smile.

"That reminds me, are you keeping up on your own training?" Fi asks.

"I am," Rose says confidently.

"I know you shoot, but what about exercising?" Fi asks.

"Daily," Rose says, "In fact I was doing push-ups when I got a knock at my door to come here."

"So that's why you took a while getting here," Fi says.

"The dude looked really uncomfortable when I answered the door, so I had to change before coming down," Rose says.

"Do I want to know?" Fi asks.

"Tank top and shorts," Rose says looking annoyed.

Fi looks confused for a moment, "Ah, you're still very young compared to everyone here. That was probably it. Anyway," Fi says, bringing the topic back to training, "Have you worked on any hand to hand stuff?"

"I know the basics from when my father was training my brother," Rose says.

"How much of the basics?" Fi asks.

"Balance and momentum stuff," Rose says.

"Okay, so you can throw people around, that's good. Have you considered learning more?" Fi asks.

"I," Rose pauses, "I don't know."

"Think about it then let me know," Fi says.

"How much do you know?" Rose asks.

"Um, stances and punching," Fi says.

"Oh," Rose says, sounding a little unsatisfied.

"I didn't care to learn anything else in the military training. Punching is pretty much all I needed," Fi says, defending himself.

"That why you use guns? Keep a distance?" Rose asks.

"I already told you why I prefer guns. Why I don't use swords," Fi says, remembering the traumatizing event.

"Oh yeah. You killed a home intruder with a sword. Sorry, it's been awhile," Rose says.

"Not long enough," Fi says. "Why don't you go run drills with the troops and I'll see you in the morning."

"Fi," Rose says, feeling empathy for him.

"You know, I shut my feelings off when everything happened. I started to feel a bit around you and Rand. Emotions have just slowly been creeping up in me since we met," Fi pauses for a moment. "It's overwhelming."

"All the more reason we should be together right now," Rose says softly.

"No," Fi says back calmly. "Memories are coming back… feelings I tried to bury. I need some alone time."

"Are you sure?" Rose asks. "I won't leave you, I care about you too much."

Fi smiles, "I do too, Rose," Fi says, hiding a tear, as he leaves.

"Fi," Rose reaches for his arm as he walks past, but hesitates and lets him go. "See you in the morning, Fi."

"See you in the morning, Rose," Fi says, not even looking back.

Rose watches Fi leave, "I hope you're okay," she says to herself. "Not much to do except wait til morning," she says, going to the courtyard to train.

She runs drills and trains with her troops until the sun goes down, then goes to bed.

Negotiations

Rose wakes up on her own and gets prepared for the day. Badass trench coat and her trusty gun belt. She opens her door to see Fi right outside, fist up just about to knock.

"Good morning," she says.

"Good morning," he says back.

"Ready to go?" Rose asks.

"Yeah, didn't expect you to be ready," Fi says surprised.

"Yeah, well I'm getting better with mornings," Rose says.

"I see, well the scouts are back and it's our turn to negotiate," Fi informs her.

"Alright, got breakfast?" Rose asks.

"Don't you usually have snacks up here?" Fi asks, facetious.

"For the record," Rose starts all serious, "I finished it last night. I'm hungry now," she says, being sassy.

"Alright, we can grab some fruit on the way out," Fi says.

Rose smiles, "that'll do."

"Alright, let's begin the day," Fi says, as they head to the gate.

"Good morning Filip," Rose calls out, seeing Filip going up the stairs at the wall to begin his day as the night watcher passes. She gets a quick memory of her nightmare with those stairs, but it quickly passes. Not as a fear but like a memory.

"Good morning, my lady," Filip responds. "Off on another thrilling adventure?" He says, seeing Fi with her.

"We're going to meet new people," Rose says cheerfully.

"Fi, you aren't in shape to be outside the walls, are you sure?" Filip asks.

"I can walk, just a little limp now," Fi says. "I'll be fine."

"My lady, you're okay with taking him out when he's injured?" Filip asks.

"We've been out plenty of times and only found one hostile group of people, Lucious isn't a threat for the time being. We'll be fine," Rose says confidently.

"If you say so. Good luck out there, be safe," Filip says, opening the gate.

"I'm always safe," Fi says ironically, limping away.

It's now that they're outside the walls that Rose really notices Fi's limp. "Will you be able to run?" She asks, just now noticing how it is.

"I'll be fine," Fi says, looking back to her.

"I was so happy to see you on your feet again that I didn't notice your limp," Rose says.

"Well you don't need to worry about it," Fi says.

"We can postpone this a day or two for you -," Rose gets cut off.

"Rose, I appreciate the concern, but I'm fine," Fi says.

"Showing up to negotiate on an alliance with someone who's limping doesn't leave a good impression," Rose says. "It shows weakness."

Fi thinks for a moment, realizing she's right, "it could show strength too," he says, trying to convince himself.

"How?" Rose asks, annoyed and unconvinced.

"Strength that we don't," Fi starts off trying to find words to convince himself. "We don't fear what's out here," he says, gaining confidence. "Yeah, yeah, we aren't afraid of what's out here."

Rose rolls her eyes. "Just don't ruin this."

"You don't trust me?" Fi asks back.

"Last time I trusted you to be fine you ended up like this," Rose says.

"Ouch," Fi says, looking at her to see if she was joking. Upon seeing her serious face he says, "You're serious. You don't trust me?"

Rose realizes the harm her face did and apologizes, "Sorry, I didn't mean it like that."

"How did you mean it?" Fi asks sadly.

Rose struggles to find the words, opening her mouth to speak with no words coming out.

"One loss and you think I can't protect you anymore? That it?" Fi says, getting agitated.

"No, it's not that," Rose says.

"A little limp doesn't mean I can't protect you. You saw him, you know how big he is. I was fortunate enough to still be alive after fighting him," Fi says, progressively raising his voice.

"It's not that," Rose says, getting agitated.

"What is it then?" Fi demands.

"I don't need you to protect me!" Rose finally yells.

The sudden yell mixed with those words leaves Fi in shock.

"You don't need to protect me," Rose says, progressively lowering her voice from a shout to normal volume. "You and Rand get so fixated on trying to protect me that you both lost yourselves and what I love about you. Please, I'm not the helpless girl you met at the capitol. Please stay true to yourself. I don't want to have to stab you."

After a few minutes that felt like hours of silence, Fi says, "I am staying true to myself. Everything I've done has been in my character," he says in a soft voice.

"This need for revenge will get you killed," Rose says back.

"What are you talking about?" Fi asks.

"You haven't been the same since that night we met Lucious. That really worries me," Rose says. "You've been over protective, reckless, and vengeful."

"What do you want me to do?" Fi asks.

"I don't know," Rose says.

"You don't know?" Fi says, getting annoyed.

"What I know is my brother had a moment like that," Rose says. "He was a great mentor and protector until the day he killed our parents. He was never the same after that."

"You're worried I'll lose myself if I kill Lucious," Fi starts.

"No, you already had that moment," Rose says softly.

Fi looks confused, "when I fought Lucious?"

"When we found that settlement that was slaughtered," Rose says, making eye contact with Fi. "You've been different ever since. The fight with Lucious just made it worse."

"I haven't been different," Fi says in disbelief.

"You were all about helping people, now it's all about killing," Rose says.

Fi is stunned, realizing she is right. But this is part of him now. He can't end up like Rand. "I only kill when I need to. To protect others," Fi says.

"That's exactly how it started with Rand," Rose says, losing eye contact, her eyes drifting down to the ground ahead. "That's exactly how I lost my brother," she says softly.

Fi feels her pain. "I won't end up like Rand," Fi finally says.

"In which way?" Rose says in a threatening tone.

"I won't get his bloodlust," Fi says confidently. "Why do you sound threatening?"

Her tone changes to sad and regretful, "I can't do it again," she says.

"Do what again?" Fi asks.

"Kill someone I love," she says bluntly.

"I won't go down that path," Fi says, "Don't worry."

"I hope not," Rose says, ending the conversation.

Both are quiet for the remainder of the journey until Fi sees the settlement.

"There it is," Fi says, breaking the silence and pointing in a manner Rose can't see.

Rose looks ahead and sees it herself, "great, that walk was longer than I thought it would be."

"I think it was the conversation that made it feel longer," Fi says. "Anyways, we're here.

"Okay, so how are we going to play this?" Rose asks.

"Thinking we talk about safety in numbers and warn them about Lucious," Fi says.

"I don't want to start a friendship out of fear," Rose says.

"Okay, how do you want to pay this?" Fi asks.

"Maybe we start off with our strength, how we destroyed the machines. Then maybe at the close we could warn them about Lucious," Rose says.

"That is a great idea. Are we sharing our strength to get them to fear us or for them to see us as a powerful ally?" Fi asks.

"Both, but like, subtly," Rose says.

"Like boast of our achievements in a peaceful manner, but leave it open to a veiled threat if they want to oppose us," Fi clarifies.

"Exactly. We are here to help, and you can't stop us," Rose says.

"That seems very uncharacteristic of you," Fi says.

"Is it the way I worded it?" Rose asks.

"Yeah, just how you said it," Fi says.

As they approach they see armed men around the perimeter. No wall, but waist high barricades.

Fi throws his rifle to his back with his sling to show open hands.

"Eyo!" Rose calls out, once she thinks they're within ear shot.

"Look at all the guards," Fi whispers to Rose, as even more move up and aim their weapons at them.

"Worried?" Rose whispers back.

"No, excited. That's a lot of men. Wonder how many more inside," Fi whispers back.

"Stop where you are!" The guards say, once they're close enough to be heard. "State your names and business."

"Eyo," Rose repeats, "We're here on behalf of, well us, to negotiate."

"Speak up," they demand.

"I'm Fi, this is Rose, we're expected," Fi shouts back. "Here to-"

"Drop your weapons! " one guard says as another approaches them.

Fi drops his rifle and keeps his hands open and visible. Rose draws her pistol and tosses it in front of her. "We're getting these back, right?" She says.

"You'll get them back on your way out," the approaching guard says, collecting their weapons. Once their weapons are collected the guards lower their weapons. "Follow me," he says, leading them past other guards as two more follow behind. They're led to a big room with a long table.

"Ah, my negotiators I assume," a man says sitting at the head of the table.

"Indeed we are," Fi says, "It's a pleasure."

"The pleasure is all mine," the man says, standing up. "The name is Jace."

"Fi."

"Rose."

"You two look rather young, siblings I assume?" Jace asks.

"No, we're friends," Fi says. "We lead our people with great prosperity," Fi starts as they all sit.

"As do I," Jace says. "So, what kind of deal are you looking for?"

"I think sharing our great accomplishments would be beneficial ahead of any talk of peace dealings," Fi suggests.

"Alright, go on," Jace says.

"Have you heard of Havoc and Helen?" Fi starts.

"The legendary warriors? Yeah, who hasn't?" Jace responds.

"I'm their daughter," Rose says.

"Whoa, hold up," Jace says excitedly, "You're Rose, daughter of Havoc?"

"I am," Rose says with pride.

"Tell me about them! Where are they now?" Jace asks.

"Dead," Rose says, trying hard to keep her emotions in check.

"Well, I guess not everyone is who they seem," Jace says disappointed.

"My brother, Rand, he killed them," an emotional pause, "We found out they joined the machines... so we stopped them," Rose says.

Everyone stopped breathing for a moment.

"You're telling me, your brother killed the toughest warriors of our time?" Jace says, excited again. "I want to meet this man."

"He's dead too," Rose says, her voice shaking, "I killed- I had to stop him… put him down ."

"Family curse?" Jace asks.

"No," Rose snarls back.

"Well damn. So you're the only one left of your family lineage. Is that what he's here for?" Jace says, pointing to Fi.

"What? No," Fi says.

"No, I'm just explaining," Rose starts, Jace's joke going over her head. "We destroyed the machines, we stopped the strongest warriors of our generation, and we stopped their killer. We are fully self-sufficient."

"What are you pitching to me?" Jace asks.

"As a powerful group to another, we are looking for safety in numbers. We have strong men and great training, training directly from Havoc. We have weapons and armor forged from the machines, we have an impenetrable defense, what we lack is the numbers for discovery and offense," Fi says.

"Tell me more about these weapons and armor from the machines," Jace says.

"We have removed their massive canons, they are now manned on top of our walls. Our armor can deflect any small arms round," Fi says, motioning to the chest piece he's wearing.

"Impressive. How much ammo do you have?" Jace asks. "Truly you can't have well trained soldiers without training. With ammo in such low supply these days."

Rose looks over to Fi as he starts talking, "Ammo is of no concern to us."

"No concern? How do you train?" Jace asks.

Rose quickly interjects before Fi can talk, "We send scouts out, we recently found a massive stockpile when we took out the machines."

"Impressive, you find these stockpiles often?" Jace asks.

"Every place we tracked the machines to had an armory," Rose lies.

Fi was first confused, but now understands. He almost gave up their secret bullet forge. He watches as Rose totally manipulates the guy, feeding him exactly what he wants to know without really telling him anything.

"Alright, you have my attention. Let's get back to the safety in numbers," Jace says. "Have you met anyone hostile out there recently?"

Rose is thinking about this, when Fi speaks bluntly, "We have. He has murdered many, I tried to stop him, but he overpowered me. He's a big guy with a lot of people."

"Sounds dangerous," Jace says.

"Yeah, I almost had him. Then his people flooded the room, ruining the fight," Fi says.

"How strong are they?" Jace asks.

"We found a town they massacred, the shots didn't look too accurate. They make up for that with their numbers," Fi says.

"Massacred?" Jace asks, concerned.

"We found farmland with some small buildings around it massacred. No casings from the buildings, these guys didn't even have guns to shoot back. I went inside and found bodies hiding with a gunshot to the head. These people were executed," Fi says.

Jace is visibly shaken hearing this, "You are positive that was from the same people?"

"Lucious confirmed it himself when I brought it up," Fi says.

"Lucious, that guy's name?" Jace asks.

"Yes, I want to kill him, he's a threat to everyone that isn't a slave to him," Fi says.

"We're working on peace right now," Rose says, quickly interjecting. "We don't want war, we want to unite as many people as we can so we can live in peace."

"I want him dead for his crimes," Fi says, "Rose here doesn't."

"Noble, or naive," Jace says. "And right now you're building an army to face this, this Lucious?"

"We want people aware of the threat and united. A threat against one is a threat against all kind of deal," Rose says.

"Sounds like you just want people to throw at your problem. You think I'll be sending my men out there for you?" Jace asks.

"We're not looking for war, we're looking for peace," Rose says.

"You're looking for pawns to wage a war with to achieve peace," Jace says, getting irritated.

Rose looks at Fi feeling defeated. Fi meets her gaze, then says, "We want long term peace and security, we want to avoid this war any way possible. Having an overwhelming force can help make sure this doesn't lead to a war."

"Okay, I can see that," Jace says. "I'll think about it. How can I keep in touch?"

Rose smiles, "do you have a radio?"

"We do not, not since the emp wiped everything out. How did you guys get radios?" Jace asks.

"Emp?" Rose asks, confused.

"electromagnetic pulse," Jace says. "It fries everything running on electricity."

"I know what it does, I mean what are you talking about an emp?" Rose asks back.

"You guys haven't noticed there's no power?" Jace asks skeptically.

Fi looks at Rose confused, she shares the same expression.

"You guys don't even know there's no power, you're lying to me about something," Jace states.

"We're not lying," Rose quickly says.

"We've gone from ruin to ruin until we finally set up in the base that Havoc ordered the machines from. It must have emp shielding, we have power," Fi says.

"You have power?" Jace asks excitedly.

"Yeah, I wasn't aware that was a problem elsewhere," Rose adds.

"What do you use?" Jace asks.

"Just lights and our main computer," Fi says. "It's like a table size map that updates in real time."

"And laundry," Rose adds.

"So you have hot water?" Jace asks.

"Yeah," Rose says.

"Damn. That oughta be nice," Jace says. "Okay, but back to the radios."

"Removed from machines we scrapped," Fi says. "We have two working ones, one for scouts and one for home base."

"Okay, well you know where I live, as a show of trust, can you tell me where you live?" Jace asks.

"I can show you a map," Fi says, looking back to Rose for her non verbal confirmation. Rose smiles back, so Fi reaches into his pocket and removes his hand drawn map in the weather proof bag.

"Wonderful, I'll send a few guys over within two days to tell you of my answer," Jace says.

"Alright, we'll await your arrival," Rose says.

"If you don't mind, I'd like a copy of that map, just so my guys don't get lost on the way," Jace asks.

"Um, sure," Fi says, feeling a little uncertain, but going ahead to show trust.

After Jace copies the map Fi says, "If there's nothing else, we'll take our leave now."

"You said you had a surplus of ammunition, would you be open to trading for it?" Jace asks.

"That would be a condition within an alliance," Rose says.

"You've just about made up my mind," Jace says. "You can take your leave, you'll get your weapons back on your way out. Farewell."

"Farewell," Rose says.

"It's been a pleasure," Fi says, heading out, following the soldier that is holding onto their weapons.

Once they leave their base the soldier they're following turns around and hands them their weapons back. "Thank you for your cooperation, have a nice day," he says.

"Thanks," Rose says, checking the chamber of her pistol then holstering it.

"Great place, would visit again," Fi says, chamber checking then putting his rifle on his back.

"We look forward to it," the soldier says, stepping aside waiting for them to leave.

"I think that went well," Fi says, as they start their long walk home.

Fi takes a quick glance back to see the soldiers using what looks like a radio. This confuses him but not enough to bring it up to Rose.

"I think this went very well," Rose says happily.

"Did we tell them a little too much?" Fi wonders aloud.

"Probably. You almost told him all of our secrets. We can't be telling anyone about our ammo situation," Rose says sternly. "We don't have the manpower to fend off attackers yet."

"Right, yeah. I was just in the negotiation thought and didn't think of how vulnerable we would look," Fi says.

"Yeah, I know," Rose says.

Jace's Deal

The next morning there's a knock on Rose's door, a lot earlier than Fi usually wakes her up.

"Rose, get up!" Fi calls through her door. "A lot of people are approaching our wall, we need to be out there," Fi shouts. Rose runs out in her nightgown with her pistol in hand.

Fi runs down the hall, down the stairs, across the courtyard to the wall just in time for the people to be in shouting distance. Fi notices they are armed but not aiming their weapons, unlike Fi's people, everyone is on the wall aiming their weapons at these unknown people.

"Far enough," Fi shouts, "State your name and business!"

"We are here on Jace's behalf, he accepts your terms," one man shouts back.

"That's good to hear, now, why are there so many of you and well armed?" Fi calls back.

"Jace requests you train us," the man shouts back.

Finally Rose catches up with Fi at the wall, "What I miss?"

"Jace sent people for us to train," Fi says back.

Rose makes a confused face, "His people were very well trained, you think this is a trap?" Rose asks.

"A trap?" Fi repeats her word so she'll elaborate.

"Send armed men into our home to discover our weaknesses," Rose elaborates.

"I don't think so, but I didn't even consider that a possibility. I think Jace wants to see how powerful we are. We puffed out our chest and he wants to see how much we exaggerated," Fi says.

"So what are we going to do?" Rose asks.

"Let them in and train them a bit. See what they know and show them what we do," Fi says to Rose, then turning his attention to Filip. "Open the gate."

They mingle for a bit as Fi gives them a tour of their base while Rose goes back to her room to change. Fi helps them set up a temporary shelter for while they're there between the personal quarters and the courtyard. Fi trains them himself.

They are pretty well organized, their weapons are similar to what they use, armor looks like just thick fabric padding, good for blunt force not much else.

Rose and Fi spend the day training and running drills with Jace's people. Some are very well trained but seem to hide it.

The Fight

Rose is working out in her room swinging her sword around. Working on the foot work and muscles when there's a knock on her door. She rests her sword against her bed to answer it.

"Hey Oscar," she says.

"Rose, have you decided on sparring?" Oscar asks.

"I have," Rose says. "When do you want to?"

"I'm ready right now," Oscar says.

"Come on in then," Rose says, opening the door wider.

"In your room?" Oscar asks nervously.

"What's wrong with that?" Rose asks.

"I um. It's a little small. Wouldn't want to break anything," Oscar says

"Do you have a better idea?" Rose asks.

"Courtyard," Oscar says.

"In front of everyone?" Rose asks.

"Everyone should know how well their leader fights," Oscar says.

"I don't want to disappoint anyone. I'm not my brother," Rose says.

"I'm not either, they don't need to see you win every fight. They just need to see that you do fight," Oscar says.

"I don't know," Rose says, remaining unconvinced.

"It will help. I could go easy and let you win if you want," Oscar says. "Just put on a good show and let everyone see you're a fighter."

Rose thinks for a moment, "I don't need you to let me win."

"I didn't mean it like that," Oscar says.

"I'll do it," Rose says, "you can start out easy, but don't hold back."

"My lady, I wouldn't have it any other way," Oscar says smiling. "Put some clothes on."

"I am wearing clothes," Rose says, looking down at her workout attire.

"You don't want me holding back, this is going to hurt, for both of us. You really shouldn't have any exposed skin," Oscar says.

"I'm fully covered," Rose says looking down at her torso.

"Thin fabric, at least put on a thick coat to protect your arms. That's all I'm looking for here," Oscar says.

"Okay," Rose goes to her closet and pulls out a new purple coat she hasn't worn before.

"Okay. That's better," Oscar says.

"Thanks," Rose says, smiling.

"After you, my lady," Oscar says, being a gentleman stepping aside for her.

"Alright, let's go," Rose says, walking past Oscar and out to the courtyard. There they see two soldiers already sparring with the wooden swords they recently made.

      Rose and Oscar wait patiently for the duel to end. Both fighters are slowing down with heavy breathing. The fight is coming to an end. Finally one raises his sword over his head to drop down, the other times his dodge to barely miss the strike then thrusts his sword into the other's abdomen. Ending the duel with an applause from the rest of the troops watching.

      Both men shake hands, the victor turns to the crowd to see Rose watching.

      "I didn't realize you were watching," the victor says with a bow. "Hope you were entertained."

      "That was a good show," Rose says, walking towards him with Oscar by her side.

      The victor looks confused seeing them both walk towards him, "Hi, um, what's going on?"

      "You put on a great show, Oscar and I are the encore," Rose says.

      "You're a fighter?" The man says surprised.

      "My brother showed me some stuff, I'm nowhere near him, but Oscar wanted to put on a show. Show you guys what kind of a leader I am," Rose says, reaching out for the sword.

      "My lady, as awesome as that sounds," he holds the sword back from her grasp, "You have nothing to prove. We all respect you as our leader."

      "I have everything to prove," she counters, reaching further for the sword.

      "I'm sorry you feel that way," he says, handing over the sword.

This hits Rose deep, *do I have anything to prove?*

"This isn't about proving anything, she's here to train with us," Oscar says. "Rose leads by example."

Rose smiles, watching Oscar get the sword from the guy that lost.

Oscar steps away from her, "Best two of three?"

"Yes," Rose says, squaring up to Oscar.

"Ready?" Oscar shouts.

"Ready," Rose shouts back.

Oscar gets into a defensive stance then shouts a battle cry and charges Rose. Rose quickly raises her sword to block his strike. Oscar moves fast, striking back and forth, weakening Rose's defense with every strike. He's stronger.

Rose gets pushed back little by little with each hit she blocks, finally she sees an opening, she glides her blade just below his, hitting the guard with an upwards motion forcing his sword up - and his arms then stabbing him with the wooden tip.

"You're strong, I'm fast," she says with a big smile.

The crowd cheers.

"Well done," Oscar says, clenching the impact. "Ow, that was a good strike."

"Thank you," Rose says, with a slight bow.

"Alright, back to the center," Oscar says, walking back.

First time Rose has battled with a sword since everything happened, she's feeling very confident. Maybe it's being in a dueling circle that brings back the memories. Maybe she learned more than she thought.

"Ready?" Oscar shouts.

"Ready," Rose shouts back.

Rose tries a style her brother used, the berserker rush. She holds the sword over her head and charges with her own battle cry. Oscar moves his sword low, going for an abdomen shot, just as predicted. She swings her sword down from the opposite side to collide with Oscar's sword, her momentum overpowering his strength, causing him to stagger. Using the remainder of her momentum, she slams her shoulder into him, knocking him to the ground. Her plan worked, until she realizes she's on the ground too. She was too focused on getting him off balance she lost hers as well. She starts getting up until the tip of a sword is pressed lightly against her chin. She looks up to see Oscar already on his feet. He won this round.

"That was an interesting round," Oscar says, lowering his sword and offering a hand to Rose.

Rose takes his hand, "my brother called it the berserker rush."

"You did very well, just need to work on your own footwork," Oscar says, pulling Rose to her feet.

"Yeah, you were supposed to be the only one falling," Rose says, walking back for the final round.

"Alright, match point, let's give them a good show," Oscar says. "Ready?"

"Ready."

This time Rose is calm and calculating. She walks towards Oscar, while he cautiously walks closer. Rose points her sword towards Oscar, he points back. They continue until they're in striking distance, their swords scraping against one another. Rose takes the first strike, lunging, Oscar blocks it with ease. But Rose loosened her grip for that lunge, knowing how he'd block it, so she never lost control of it, quickly swings it back towards Oscar's front. Oscar deflects it to the other side, Rose does the same trick to again from that side now. Oscar barely blocks it. She grins and gets over confident. *You're fast, but I'm faster,* she swings a fast three hit combo going from his thigh up to his chest, but Oscar blocks each hit. The final block was a parry in which he spun around and slammed his blunt sword into Rose abdomen, just below her ribs. She drops her sword and slumps over in pain.

"Oooohhh," the crowd felt that blow too.

Oscar turns back to Rose to see her down on her hand knees clutching her stomach, "was that too hard?" He asks, apologetically.

"I can't breathe," she says, struggling to make words.

Oscar kneels down next to her with his hand on her back, "Are you okay?"

Rose's panting is getting deeper and slowing down. "Why did you hit me so hard?"

"I… Uh… You didn't want me to hold back," Oscar says.

Fi comes limp running out from the living area with his rifle in hand. "Oscar, why did you do that?!" He yells.

"I didn't mean to hit that hard, we were dueling," Oscar says, defending himself.

"Be gone," Fi shouts.

"I'm sorry," Oscar says, his face completely red as he rushes to his quarters out of guilt and embarrassment.

Fi throws his rifle to his back and runs next to Rose. "Are you okay?"

"Yeah," she says, lifting her shirt to inspect the impact.

"The party's over, back to what you were doing," Fi says.

"Help me to my room?" Rose asks.

"Of course," Fi says.

"We were dueling, I thought I did pretty well," Rose says, leaning against Fi while he leans against her.

"You did great," Fi says, walking her to the living quarters.

"You saw?" Rose asks.

"I saw the whole thing. You did great first two rounds," Fi says.

"I didn't see you out here," Rose says.

"I was watching from the doorway. Everyone looked impressed," Fi says, entering the living quarters.

"How impressed are they seeing me get carried away?" Rose says, letting go of Fi and trying to walk on her own.

"You just got smacked full force by a guy a lot bigger than you, I think they'll be impressed seeing you get up quickly," Fi says, trying to comfort her as they walk to her room.

"He just got caught up in the duel, I don't blame him," Rose says.

"I know, I don't either," Fi says.

"Why were you really upset with him if you knew it was an accident?"

Fi takes a breath, "I saw you hurt and I just went into overdrive. I'm sorry, I shouldn't have reacted like that."

"I'm not the one you need to apologize to," Rose says, as they get to her room.

"I'll find him and apologize," Fi says. "You'll be alright here?"

"In my room?" Rose asks, confused.

"I mean, how bad is it?" Fi asks.

Rose opens the door and enters. She turns around to Fi and lifts her shirt up to show the impact.

Fi's eyes go wide as he stares at her stomach. The impact left a red line going across her abs.

Rose inspects the wound, "Just a contusion. It's sore and hurts to the touch, but doesn't appear to be anything serious." Rose looks up to meet Fi's gaze, upon seeing his face she blushes and lowers her shirt.

Fi clears his throat, "you said nothing serious, good."

Rose smiles uncontrollably.

"I um," Fi clears his throat again, "I should get going."

"You like what you saw?" Rose asks, shyly. She loves the way he looked at her, she loves him.

"I uh," Fi looks back to her, looking into her eyes. He takes a deep breath, "I need to go," he says, turning and leaving quickly.

Rose is disappointed he left, "Yeah, okay," she says to herself. She closes the door and heads to her bed. "You just need some rest. No abdominal movement for a while," Rose mumbles to herself, "Just need to rest my eyes for a second," she says, dropping her coat and laying down.

No More

Rose wakes up in a blank room, nothing around but her bed. She sits up and looks around, nothing. Not even a door. "What kind of dream is this?" She asks herself out loud.

"Not a dream. Nightmare," Summer says, appearing at the foot of Rose's bed.

"What kind of nightmare?" Rose asks calmly.

"The kind that you don't wake up from," Summer hisses threateningly.

Rose remains calm, "No it isn't. If you have something to say, go ahead and say it, then leave."

"Oh look at you, so confident now. You think you're safe?" Summer asks.

"I am. I'm not alone," Rose says, as Rand appears in her room by her bed.

"Sister," Rand says, greeting Rose. "Summer, how many times do I need to kill you?" He says, turning his attention to Summer.

Summer pulls out the knife she threw at Rand and responds, "I was just thinking the same thing."

"No- not in my room," Rose says, her words piercing reality itself. Now the three of them stand in the courtyard.

"Doesn't matter to me where you die," Summer says.

"Just what I was thinking," Rand says back, drawing his sword in a defensive stance.

"You can't kill me, you're already dead," Rose's words cut through the emptiness, disintegrating Summers' weapon.

Summer gasps in fear, she no longer has any control over Rose, and they both know it. "Are you just going to execute me? Like brother like sister," Summer taunts.

"No. I'm sorry for what my brother did to you," Rose starts, stepping towards Summer. "But I'm not my brother, I forgive you." Upon saying those words Summer vanishes along with the guilt of what happened to her.

"Brother," Rose starts.

"I'm here sister," Rand says back.

"I'm so sorry," she opens with. "I'm sorry I killed you, I'm sorry for how I treated you, -."

Rand interrupts her, "It's fine. The past is in the past.

"No it's not fine," her eyes filled with tears once again. "I told you you can't protect me and I felt safer with Fi."

"Fi is a great man, I trust him too," Rand comforts.

"I pushed you too much. It's my fault," Rose says, overwhelmed with guilt.

"No it's not," Rand stops her again, putting his hand on her shoulder. "I got overwhelmed with all the evil in the world, I let it take hold of me. I used it for strength and it eventually overwhelmed me."

"I should've been a better sister," Rose says, refusing to let go of that guilt.

"Look around, these people respect you," upon saying that the courtyard fills with life. "Fi respects you. You now have more than I ever did. You earned it. You worked hard for this. This is yours. Don't let the guilt of what might have been ruin what you have," Rand says, looking around at her Home.

Rose smiles, "You're right brother. Thank you for everything. You always know what to say."

"No, Rose," Rand disagrees. "You already know what you need, you just don't have courage to do it yourself. You just want someone to tell you first."

Rose tries to defend herself but he's right - she's right? Her conscience is right.

"You're afraid if an idea doesn't work out people will see you as a failure," Rand says, being her own in-dream therapist. "You see, everyone fails. People don't judge when they see failure, they judge on how well you overcome that failure."

His words - her thoughts hit deep. Her deep fears of inadequacy of her parents and brother leave her feeling like she can never live up to their level. Her family has set such a high bar that she fears she will never reach.

"Sister, don't worry about us. Focus on yourself. You're already a better leader than we ever were," Rand says. "You will raise that bar eventually. You just need a push-," upon saying that he vanishes, the emotional turmoil she's feeling is finally enough to wake her up. She dwells on her family until morning, lying awake in her bed.

Him Again

"Rose!" There's a loud knock on her door.

"What is it?" Rose calls back.

"Lucious is here," Fi says through the door.

"Great," Rose says sarcastically.

"Could be great, he said he's here to negotiate," Fi says.

"That's not like you," Rose says, confused.

"Well, I uh, saw the error of my ways," Fi says unconvincingly.

Rose gets up and moves to the door, she opens it to see Lucious. She's speechless, she wasn't expecting him to be at her door.

"It's good to see you too," Lucious says.

"Lucious," Rose says, passive aggressively.

"Rose," Lucious says back, mimicking her tone.

"Why don't we go back to the courtyard," Rose says.

"Why don't you put on more clothes," Lucious responds.

"Are you going to give a girl some privacy?" Rose asks indignantly.

"Yeah, this is just weird for me. You may see me as a bad guy, but I'm not one of *those* bad guys," he says.

Rose rolls her eyes and closes the door. She looks down to see she's still wearing her workout attire. *It'll be fine with a coat*, she thinks as she looks back for the coat she took off before laying in bed. She puts the coat on then opens the door to see Lucious still right there.

"Yeah I guess that works," Lucious says. "Nice coat."

"Courtyard," Rose says.

"My lady, I find personal negotiations feel more intimate in personal rooms," Lucious says.

"Courtyard, now," Rose says.

"Well look at you giving me orders like that," Lucious says in a surprisingly charming way. "I hold all the power and you still try to boss me around."

"You bring out the worst in me," Rose says sternly.

"Yeah I get that a lot," Lucious chuckles to himself. "You got mighty big balls talking to me like that. Though I guess I shouldn't expect anything less coming from your family. If you were anyone else, I would've killed you many times over," Lucious says.

"Yeah I got that impression," Rose snarks back.

Fi is in awe just watching Rose talk down to this big guy.

"You see, if it was your boyfriend here," Lucious says, pointing over his shoulder to Fi, "I would've killed him where he stands."

"Ready for round two?" Fi snaps back.

Without even turning to acknowledge him, "You're still hurt. You wouldn't last a minute," Lucious says.

Fi gets angry, but tries to hide it.

"You think you're a big scary man, but to me you're not," Rose starts.

"Oh you think you know me. This outta be good. Please, go on," Lucious says.

"But you're not. You're just a scared little boy with mommy issues. That's why you take orders from me. Now go to the courtyard or you don't get supper," Rose says.

"Damn," Lucious shouts holding back his laughter, "That's far from it, but man are you funny. I'm not in the habit of killing women, especially kids."

"You had no problem with Fi," Rose says.

"Fi isn't a woman or a kid," Lucious states.

"I'm seventeen," Fi says. "This kid almost killed you."

Lucious looks back, "there's no way you're seventeen. You fought with military training."

"I joined the military young, almost killed you with those skills," Fi says, being cocky.

Lucious looks conflicted, "You almost made me kill a kid," he says. The tone shocks Rose, that's the first time she's heard him be serious. "I almost killed a kid."

Rose can see the conflict in his eyes, he's serious.

"No, you almost died by a kid," Fi says.

"You look older than you are," Lucious says, getting back to his normal. "I don't mean that as a bad thing."

"I'm flattered," Fi says, crossing his arms.

"I would've thought that fight would've humbled you. You're alive because of your girlfriend. Nothing else," Lucious says. "Anyway, let's get to the negotiations. That's why I'm here after all."

"Okay. We're not kneeling or giving up our weapons," Rose says sternly.

"Yeah I remember. Best we can do right now is a truce," Lucious says. "You don't come after my people, I don't go after your people."

"We've never gone after your people," Rose says.

"That's how we met, you came after me," Lucious says.

"No, we were looking for others to join us. Trying to save as many people as we can," Rose says.

"From who? You said you destroyed the machines?" Lucious asks.

"We did," Rose says.

"Then why am I still seeing signs of them?" Lucious says.

"What signs?" Rose asks.

"Footprints for one. When did you say you destroyed them?" Lucious asks.

"Um," Rose tries to think back but every day since the day everything fell just seems to blend together. She can't get an accurate number. "Not too long ago."

"Well I saw new prints on my way here," Lucious says.

Rose looks worried.

"That's impossible," Fi says, "We destroyed all the machines around here. We destroyed the targeting computer too. There's no more machines."

"You sound so certain," Lucious says.

"We did," Rose says.

"Alright, anyway, I've set up territory for me and my people," Lucious says, pulling out a hand drawn map from his coat pocket. "Imagine a line from this farmland crossing north-south. Everything east is my territory, Everything west, up to you."

Rose looks suspicious at the map, *what could be so important there?*

"That's the settlement with all the farms that you executed, right?" Fi says.

"That's right. You stay out there we got no trouble," Lucious says, pointing to the map.

"You're taking a lot of space," Rose says, trying to connect the dots.

"I'm expanding. I told you, we're rebuilding civilization," Lucious says.

"And this imaginary line will remain when civilization is brought back," Rose says.

"As long as there is peace between us, " Lucious says.

Fi inspects the map looking for any kind of hidden motive. He can't find any, they already explored most of that area, it's where they first met Lucious.

"You guys can read a map right?" Lucious asks. "You're out over here," he says, pointing off the map towards the west.

"We know how to read maps," Rose answers.

"You both seem to be lost looking at this. Don't tell me it's my drawing," Lucious jokes.

"Looking for a hidden motive," Fi says.

"Hidden motive?" Lucious repeats with a chuckle.

"Is there a reason you want that area?" Rose asks.

"I mean, it's within my half of the halfway point between our main bases," Lucious says.

"You know, you know where we live, but we haven't seen where you live," Rose says.

"You don't need to know," Lucious says.

"What are you hiding?" Fi asks.

"Not hiding anything," Lucious says.

"How can we have a truce based on trust when you don't give us a reason to trust you?" Rose asks.

"You want trust? You're alive," Lucious says, pointing to Rose. "And you're alive," he says pointing at Fi. "I had enough opportunities to kill both of you. Hell I have the manpower to flatten your base. If you want trust, your breathing should be enough."

"You think that's how you build trust?" Rose pulls out her pistol to disengage the safety and pull the hammer back. She then points it at Lucious's head, "Do you trust me?"

"You're not gonna pull the trigger," Lucious says.

Fi is speechless, that's something not even he would even consider doing.

"Why's that?" Rose hisses.

"Everyone knows I'm here. If I don't return, everyone you care about will die while you watch, then you," Lucious says.

Rose looks deep into his eyes then safes her pistol, dropping the hammer, "I didn't kill you. Now you have to trust me," she says.

Lucious smirks, "Well played," he then points just off the map. "Here," he looks up to them, "Should I expect guests soon?"

Rose looks at Fi, he's very focused studying the map.

"No, don't care where you are," Fi says, "Just as long as you're not here."

"Something we both agree on," Lucious says. "You can swing by to chat anytime."

"That's near the old capital," Fi says, trying to get an estimate with the distance.

"The capital? That's destroyed." Rose says.

"It is," Lucious says.

Rose and Fi look at each other, practically reading each other's minds for a moment.

"I accept your terms," Rose finally says.

"As do I," Fi says.

"Wonderful, I hope we see each other again… I do love these talks," Lucious says.

"I don't," Fi says.

"Don't got to be hurtful about it," Lucious teases.

"Looks like your home is quite far away and it's getting late," Rose says, giving him a hint.

"You're right, I should get out of your hair," Lucious says, taking the hint. "I thank you for your hospitality," he says with a slight bow. "Until next time."

"Until then," Rose says, finding herself amused.

"If there is a next time," Fi says.

Lucious turns to head out, taking the same path he took coming in. Rose and Fi follow close behind. They get out to the courtyard to see Oscar staring at some of the soldiers.

"Oscar, did our guests behave themselves?" Rose asks, seeing him fixated on a few.

"Remember those people I met a few days ago?" Oscar asks back without even turning his gaze.

"Who?" Rose asks suspiciously.

"The group of wanderers I found scouting," Oscar elaborates.

"Oh yeah, are they here?" Rose asks.

"They're here," Oscar confirms.

"Here with Lucious?" Rose asks.

"Yup. They came in with him," Oscar says, saddened. "I really thought they could be allies."

"Well, at least they aren't enemies," Rose says.

"Yeah, you're right," Oscar says with a sigh. "Rose, sorry about earlier."

"It's fine," Rose says, forgiving him.

"You fought very well, after you got me the first round, then knocked me down the second, I didn't see you as a small girl attacking me, I saw you as an equal. Equal skill, I had to be fast for an opening. I really didn't mean to hit you that hard," Oscar says.

Rose looks up at him, all she wanted was to be seen as an equal, and she was. But that led to her getting hit with an equal force of someone twice her size, maybe not the best form of equality. "I appreciate that," she says after much thinking. "I accept your apology," she says with a smile.

Fi is right behind her watching this interaction with a smile.

"That's good, I uh, got things to do. See you around," Oscar says, turning to leave.

"I told you," Fi says to Rose as Oscar walks off. The sudden line startles Rose. "They see you as an equal."

"Yeah," Rose says.

"That's what you wanted, right?" Fi asks.

"Yeah, but I don't think I'm ready for the equal force yet," Rose says.

"What do you mean?" Fi asks.

"That hit, it was meant for an equal of someone almost twice my size," Rose says.

"Yeah, it did leave a mark," Fi says. "That's what armor is for, you weren't wearing it."

"Well first of all, my armor stops at my ribs, that hit still would've impacted my stomach. Second, I didn't think to. The armor is still pretty new to me," Rose says.

"Right," Fi says, "Understandable."

Give Peace A Chance

Rose's people flourish with their new found peace with Lucious. For the better part of a year, they have brought in more people to their base, which now feels like a home. People who were displaced by the machine attack, people driven from their homes by bandits, and just some vagabonds. Everyone joined together to build small houses for the newcomers.

No one dares oppose them. They have a formidable force now and a treaty with Lucious, which they lie about. They tell everyone it's an alliance, if they mess with them Lucious will come to their aid.

Not much else happens, they train more people, they feed more people, they build more homes outside the wall and work on a second wall around the new homes.

Rose stands at the balcony with Fi, overlooking the gate, the homes outside the gate, and the construction of the second wall.

"This is nice."

As Rose is focused on the housing effort, Fi is focused on the training. "This is. We have more trained soldiers than ever before," he says.

"I mean all the people we've helped," Rose says.

"And all the people we will help," Fi responds.

"We have families here now," Rose says with pride.

"Yeah, you're no longer the youngest person here," Fi jokes.

"Not the only girl anymore," she smiles.

"Yeah, the women aren't too bad on the eyes," Fi teases.

Rose nudges Fi's shoulder with a grin.

"Hey, you know you're mine," Fi says, glancing back to Rose.

"Yours huh?" Rose says, lifting her eyebrows still smiling.

"My girlfriend," Fi quickly recovers.

"Your girlfriend huh?" Rose teases.

"Yes, my beautiful girlfriend," Fi corrects.

"Well, you're not too bad on the eyes either," she says, hugging him. During the hug she notices she's touching him, not his armor. She pulls back and opens the coat he's wearing to see his muscles showing through his shirt. "You're not wearing your armor."

"Yeah, don't need to within these walls," Fi says.

Rose has noticed Fi's change during this peace. His eyes are filled with light again, he seems happier. Happier than she's ever seen him.

"You don't have your rifle either?" Rose notices next.

"Look at all these people here. Our people. We finally have peace," Fi says, gesturing out over the courtyard.

Look how he changed. How he saved himself, Rose thinks. *From the brink of losing himself to regaining his humanity and finding peace.* Rose looks upon Fi, sun glowing behind him. Fi looks so much more attractive to Rose now. *He's even stronger than brother, he's a keeper.*

Rose can't help herself and plants a kiss on Fi's cheek.

Fi smiles, "What was that for?" He asks, facing Rose.

"Do I need a reason?" Rose smirks.

"A reason for kissing my cheek," Fi clarifies, leaning forward and delivering a kiss on her lips.

Rose sees it coming when he leaned down and kisses him back, wrapping her arms around behind his neck. Peace. Love. Belonging, everything she needs, she has with him.

Safe. Loved. Belonging, everything he needs he has with her. Fi wraps his arms around her back, after the kiss they both stay in each other's arms gazing into each other's eyes.

After what seemed like an eternity of soul searching, Fi finally says, "I wonder what Lucious is doing."

"What?" Rose asks, ruining her smile.

"Surely he's up to something," Fi adds.

"Stay here," Rose says, holding him tighter.

"I'm not going anywhere," Fi says.

"Stay in the here and now, with me," Rose clarifies. "Forget about him. We are happy here, right? We have peace."

"But for how long? How long until he brings back a bigger force?" Fi asks.

"We're building up defenses too. Don't think about that," Rose begs once more.

"I know we're safe here, but we can never be too careful," Fi says.

Rose looks aside and backs away from Fi, looking over the balcony once more before heading to her room.

Fi sighs. "Sorry. Shouldn't have brought him up," his words fall on deaf ears as Rose doesn't respond and continues to her room.

On her way to her room, she walks past a soldier.

"Hey, Rose?" he asks as he turns to face her.

"Yeah?" Rose responds, facing him.

"I um, do you remember me?" he asks nervously.

Rose takes a long look at the young man's face, "You look familiar," she says.

"I was one of the first new recruits. When we met, I remember seeing a child walk up to me wearing blood stained clothes telling me she's the leader. I doubted you then," the man says.

"Oh I remember you," Rose says with a half smile.

"I need to apologize, I didn't know you then. But I do now. You're a great leader,' he says, trying to smile through his guilt.

Rose smiles more, "That means a lot," she says.

"I hope I didn't give you any doubt," he says.

"None at all," Rose says. "I have Fi with me, he takes all my doubt away."

"That's good. Just so you know, everyone respects you. There is no doubt from us," he says, referring to the soldiers.

Rose looks up into his eyes with an even bigger smile, "Thank you. That means a lot."

"We'll follow you anywhere," he says.

"Thank you," Rose responds.

"See you around," he says, starting to turn away.

"See you," Rose says happily as she continues to her room.

Bad Idea

"This really isn't a good idea," Rose whispers to Fi.

"You're as curious as I am with why he set up the territory here," Fi says back.

"I just wanted a peak, we can't get caught out here," Rose whispers.

"We're in the trees, no one will see us," Fi says back.

They arrive at the treeline just outside the destroyed fuel depot where they were attacked by snipers.

"Why would Lucious want this?" Fi asks rhetorically.

"Yeah, he already knows we blew it up," Rose says.

"He knows it was us?" Fi asks surprised.

"Yeah, it was when he hinted at having spies," Rose says. "I forgot about his spies, we really shouldn't be out here."

"Don't worry, that's why we didn't tell anyone where we were going," Fi reassures her. Fi stops in his tracks, "That looks abnormal," he says, moving towards a tree with a big leaf pile underneath.

"What?" Rose looks at the tree, just looks like a normal tree with a pile of leaves.

"This looks like a -," before Fi can finish his sentence he gets lifted up by a snare catching both his feet slamming him into the tree. The snare hangs him upside down just over Rose's head, once he reaches the top his arms slumped downward, his rifle sling slides right off his back and lands by Rose's feet.

Rose panics drawing her pistol, she looks around frantically for anyone to be watching.

"A trap," Fi says, finishing his sentence. "Well good thing I'm not alone."

"I don't think anyone's nearby," Rose says, starting to calm down. "How do I get you down?"

"You can start by holstering your pistol. Won't need that. Let's see how much weight this snare can take," Fi says, reaching his arms down to Rose.

"Just pull?" Rose asks, after holstering her pistol.

"Grab my hands and pull," Fi confirms.

"Okay," Rose says, reaching up and barely reaching his hands. She pulls with all her strength, nothing.

"Lift your feet off the ground," Fi suggests.

"I am," Rose says, hanging from Fi's grip.

Fi is getting dizzy, the blood is pooling in his head, he drops Rose.

"Oof," Rose makes a noise falling on her butt.

"Sorry, I- I'm getting dizzy," Fi says.

"Do you have a knife? Can you untie yourself?" Rose asks.

"I carry a gun so I don't need a knife," Fi says, then struggling to do a sit up. "No, no I can't. Too heavy."

Rose watches as Fi's eyes start to flutter, he's struggling to stay awake, she needs to act fast. She looks around and sees a tree next to Fi looks climbable.

"Hang on Fi," Rose says, getting ready to climb the tree. She gets right up next to it, next thing she knows, she's upside down. The upward fall knocked the wind out of her and smacking her head on the tree, it takes her a moment to realize what happened.

Fi sees Rose dangling next to him, "Uh oh. Can you get out?"

"I better," Rose says, doing a sit up and reaching her feet. "I can't untie it." The rope is too tight around her ankles to slip out.

"Rose, I can't focus," Fi says, his eyes closing.

"Fi stay with me," Rose says, panicking. She scours her pockets for anything to cut the rope. Her head is filling with blood, she's getting dizzy. Her coordination is slowing down. She gets to her holster, draws her pistol and takes aim at the rope around her ankles. She doesn't have a shot, she looks to Fi, aims just above his feet. Her hands shake as she grips the trigger, the muzzle sways down to Fi's feet. She quickly releases the trigger, seeing the hammer is halfway back, she tries again, aiming at the rope. Her vision gets blurry. Everything goes black.

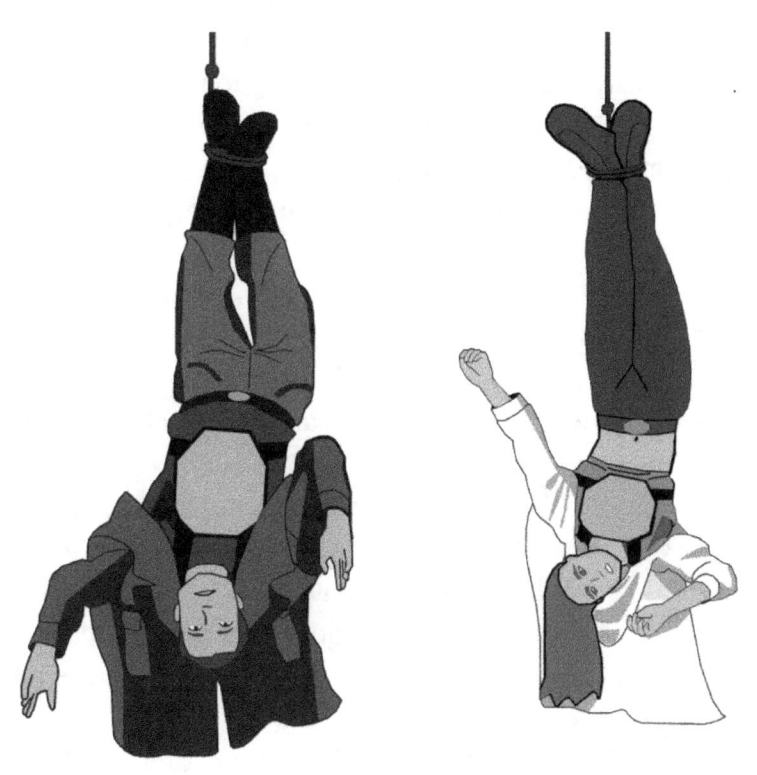

    Rose wakes up on the ground next to Fi, her head is still spinning. "Fi," she calls out, thinking it was him that eventually freed them. "Fi," she calls out again, seeing he's not moving, she wonders who got them down. That's when she notices she can't move. She's bound at her wrists and ankles with her arms behind her back.

    "This one's awake," a man says behind Rose.

"Who are you?" Rose asks, struggling to move.

"Quit your squirming, you ain't getting out of this," he says, scooping her up on his shoulder.

"Uof," Rose makes an involuntary noise when she's dropped on the man's shoulder.

"You're leaving me with the guy?" Another man says.

"That's your trap, this was my trap," the first guy says back.

"Garrett, this guy looks like he weighs as much as I do, how am I supposed to carry him back?" The second man says.

"Well, you better start then. I'm not waiting," Garrett says.

"I hate you," the man says.

"I know Dave, I know," Garrett says back. "Get your guy and let's go. I'll carry their guns, make it a little easier for you."

"Gee, a little rifle with a sling, that means a lot," Dave says.

Rose is more awake now, "Why did you set those traps?" She demands.

"Why did you fall for them?" Garrett asks back.

"Where are you taking us?" Rose demands again.

"Look sweetie, I'm not answering any of your questions. Why don't you be quiet like your friend there," Garrett says.

"If you don't release me, I'll -," Rose starts.

"You'll what? Squirm more? You're not getting out of my knots. Trust me," Garrett says.

"I will get out of this, and when I do," Rose starts, getting interrupted again.

"You're just a small defenseless child. There's nothing you can do. Not without this guy at least," Garrett says.

"I'm Rose, daughter of," she gets interrupted again.

"Is he your older brother protecting you, or a boyfriend?" Garrett asks.

"Older brother is my guess," Dave says.

"He's not my brother," Rose says. "We are," Rose gets interrupted yet again.

"Don't care," Garrett says. "If I wanted you to speak I would tell you to."

"What's your name?" Dave asks.

"My name is Rose, I am the leader of -," Rose gets interrupted again.

"You were only asked your name," Garrett says. "If you keep talking you're going to be silenced."

"You would kill me for that?" Rose says.

"I've killed for less," Garrett says.

"I have powerful friends," Rose starts again.

"Alright, knock her out," Garrett says, letting Dave get behind him.

"You wouldn't dare," were her last words.

Dave grabs the back of Rose's head and slams her face into Garrett's back armor plate, knocking her out.

"Rose? Rose wake up," that's Fi's voice.

Rose opens her eyes, everything is blurry and her head hurts even worse now.

She still can't move her arms or legs, she's laying on the ground again, her head and shoulders propped up by something.

"You're awake, that's a relief," Fi says, with a sigh of relief.

"Fi?" Rose asks, her eyes opening and closing against her will. She feels something on her cheek, something warm. It's a hand, she looks over as her eyes finally focus, is Fi's hand. She's propped up on his legs.

"What happened?" Fi asks.

"Hey, I should be asking you that," Rose says back.

"I didn't wake up with blood on my face, did they drop you?" Fi asks.

"No, he hit me," Rose says.

"Who did?" Fi asks.

"I don't know. Everything is blurry," Rose says.

Rose looks up to Fi, that's when she notices he isn't wearing his armor. "You were wearing your armor, right?" Rose asks.

"I was, yeah. They took everything," Fi says.

Rose looks down at herself, yup. Everything is gone but her shirt and pants. "Those scumbags took my coat," she says angrily.

"At least we're together," Fi says.

Rose snuggles closer to him, "where are we?"

"Some kind of cell, no one's guarding, but we're locked in," Fi says, looking at the bars.

"Wait, your hands aren't tied?" Rose notices out loud.

"I managed to untie myself after I woke up. I was waiting for you to wake up to untie you," Fi says.

"I'm awake," Rose says, sitting up and maneuvering her hands to Fi's lap.

"Alright, give me just a second," he says, untying the knot. "I was waiting for you to wake up, in case they walked in while you were still out you wouldn't be able to hide it."

"Thank you," Rose says, as soon as the rope drops. She leans forward and begins untying her ankles. "How long have you been awake?"

"I don't know, - a while, probably a few minutes," Fi says.

"Did they say anything? What do they want with us?" Rose asks, cuddling up to Fi again.

"No one was here when I woke up," Fi says.

"Can we escape?" Rose asks, leaning on Fi's shoulder.

"There's nothing in here to escape with. Even then, we'd be unarmed against however many people are out there," Fi says.

"So we just wait?" Rose asks.

"Yeah, they'll be back any minute. We can learn more about these people and what they want from there," Fi says.

"Should we make some noise to get someone in here?" Rose asks.

"Couldn't hurt. We do need answers, I do want to scope this place out before anyone sees though," Fi says, gently nudging Rose so he can get to his feet.

"Do we want them to know we're loose?" Rose asks, gathering the rope back up.

"No, good thinking," Fi says, watching Rose hide all the rope behind her.

"See anything we can use?" She says, getting up holding onto the rope behind her back with both hands.

"No windows, small empty room, one door," Fi starts, thinking out loud. "No keys, so everything must be out that door."

"So no use?" Rose asks.

"There's nothing in this room that can be used to get us out," Fi says, walking back to where he was previously sitting to sit back down.

"So loud noises?" Rose asks.

"I got an idea, pass me a piece of rope," Fi says, reaching to Rose.

Bad To Worse

Fi and Rose start yelling to get someone in the cell.
"Hey you can't keep us here!" Rose yells.
"We need to talk!" Fi adds.
After a few minutes, the door finally opens and two men walk in. Rose recognizes them instantly, it's Garrett and Dave.
"Ah you're awake," Garrett says, walking up to the cell.
"You," Rose says, glaring at Garrett.
"Me is right my dear," Garrett says unfazed.
"Why are we here?" Fi asks.
"You're here cuz we brought you here," Garrett says.
"You kidnapped us?" Fi asks.
"Yeah, I recognize both of them," Rose says.
"You do? You were awake when they grabbed us?" Fi asks.
"That one knocked me out," Rose says, pointing to Dave.
"You hit her?!" Fi says angrily.
"She was talking too much," Dave says.

"You're in our house now, what we say goes," Garrett says.

"I've fought bigger men before," Fi says, standing up with his hands still behind his back. "Bigger and uglier men," he says, trying to provoke them.

"You look a little small to be making those threats, don't you think?" Garrett says, mocking him.

"I beat Lucious in hand to hand combat, you're nothing," Fi says.

"Yeah right," the men scoff, "Lucious is alive."

"I just about killed him when he called for help," Fi says.

"Lucious doesn't call for help," the men continue to scoff at him. "At least meet the guy before you make stuff up about him."

"You know Lucious?" Rose asks.

"Who's Lucious?" Dave asks back.

Rose looks confused for a moment.

"Of course we know him," Dave says with laughter seeing how confused Rose was.

"We have an alliance with him, holding us here will bring him. You've seen his people, he won't stop until we're free," Rose says, trying to intimidate them her way.

"No you don't. You can't both tell different stories to us. First you almost killed him, now you're friends with him?" Garrett says.

"My name is Rose, sister of Rand, daughter of Havoc and Helen. We have powerful friends, we destroyed the machines and now use their weapons as our own," Rose says, trying to intimidate them again.

"No you're not," Garrett says. "You tell way too many stories."

"Let. Us. Out," Fi says.

"No. I. Won't," Garrett says, mocking him. "You see these keys?" He says, grabbing a key ring with two keys on it from his pocket. "This is the only way you're getting out, and I'm holding them," he then gets right up to the cell, dangling the keys right at the bars.

"Too bad you're tied up. You're not getting out of here unless we let you out," Dave says, approaching the bars in front of Rose. "And we ain't letting you out."

Fi looks to Rose to give the signal, "Let's get out," he says, reaching through the bars quickly wrapping the rope he tied into a noose around Garrett's neck pulling it to the side to spin him around, pinning him to the cell.

Rose gets her rope around Dave's neck in sync with Fi, she gets Dave's back to her the same way Fi does and begins strangling him.

"Open the gate now," Rose says firmly.

"Nnnnnaaahhhggg," Garrett says, tossing the keys to the side.

Fi continues to tighten his rope around Garrett's neck, "Looks like there's nothing keeping you alive now."

"Grab the keys and let us out or you'll die," Rose says firmly again.

"Aaaggh," Dave is frantically reaching for it, just barely out of his reach.

Rose could loosen her grip so he could reach the keys, but then he could escape. Instead, she tightens the rope around his neck, "Use your feet," she says calmly.

Garrett falls unconscious while Dave frantically squirms. Finally Dave kicks the keys back to the cell where Rose can reach it. She grabs the keys and tosses them to Fi, he gets the gate open as Dave passes out.

"What do we do with them?" Rose whispers.

"Tie them up," Fi says, removing the rope from Garrett's neck and tying his hands and feet together with rope going across his mouth.

Rose follows suit, mimicking everything Fi does. Including hiding the bodies in the cell. Pausing for a moment, Fi punches the one that knocked out Rose.

Fi grins admiring his handy work, a bleeding crooked nose.

"We need weapons," Rose says.

"Search em," Fi says, pulling out a large knife from Garrett's waistband.

"Got a knife," Rose says, pulling out a knife from the other's sheath.

"We need to make sure they don't get out," Fi looks at the keys then around the room. Then he gets a brilliant idea, he inserts the key in the lock, then kicks it so the teeth break off. "They aren't getting out of that."

"Fi, we need to go," Rose whispers more urgently.

"Right, I want our armor back, that'll probably be in the armory," Fi says.

"Anyone of these guys could be wearing it," Rose says.

"I don't think so. These guys caught us, I would assume the loot would go to them. Neither had guns, they probably check in everything when they enter their base," Fi says.

"That would mean we would probably only be against other unarmed people, okay. If that's true they just made this easier for us," Rose says.

"Yup. Follow my lead," Fi says, slowly peeking around the door.

"Think we can blend in or are we going to sneak around?" Rose whispers.

"They're dressed normal, not much setting them apart from us clothing wise," Fi says. "No visible markings, we may have a chance."

"Just can't be seen leaving the prison," Rose whispers.

"Right, once we have an opening, just act casual. Not sure how long until they pick us out of the crowd, but eventually someone will recognize us as not living here," Fi says.

"Yeah, on your lead," Rose whispers.

"Moving left, staying along the side of the cell, once we round the corner we can start looking for their armory" Fi whispers.

"I'm ready," Rose whispers.

"Now," Fi says, sneaking out with Rose close on his heels.

The road is completely clear just long enough for them to round the corner, there they see a whole town. Buildings still being built, people bringing in logs and setting them up in frames.

"Wow," Fi stops in awe for a moment.

"They're building?" Rose says, surprised. "They really are restoring society."

"We know now why Lucious didn't want us here," Fi says, snapping out of his trance to continue walking.

"Wait, we should find out if they're linked to Lucious," Rose says.

"They are," Fi says. "They know of Lucious, they definitely either work for him or with him."

Rose and Fi walk around a few blocks, looking in amazement seeing a big town still standing.

"There," Fi says, pointing with a nod. "Armed guards at my front right. Bet that's the armory."

"So how do we do this?" Rose asks.

"Hang here," Fi takes a quick turn and leans against a building, turning to face what he presumes is the armory.

Rose walks around to face him, her back to the armory. "What's your plan?"

"Totally outnumbered and too many civilians out for a gunfight. Let's try to get in and out. Silent knock outs only," Fi says.

"Do you think they let anyone in the armory?" Rose asks, suggesting he looks at who enters.

"Looks like," Fi says, watching as a person in casual clothes walks in no problem. "Looks like anyone is allowed in."

"So we go in, find our weapons and armor, knock out the guards, then what?" Rose asks.

"New faces walking out fully armed," Fi says, "we won't get far."

"We can climb the wall," Rose suggests, "the armory should have rope and maybe a hook or something."

"You and climbing walls," Fi teases. "The wall doesn't look too high, maybe 8 to 10 feet?" Fi estimates based on objects around the wall.

"So we don't need rope," Rose says.

"Nope. Not if you can lift me," Fi says.

"I do push-ups now, double digits," Rose jokes.

"Alright, let's do this," Fi says, walking to the armory with Rose by his side.

"Good morning," a guard says.

"Good morning," Fi repeats back.

Rose just makes eye contact with a smile and nods.

The guard watches as Rose and Fi walk into the armory. There's more guards inside, as expected.

Rose sees Fi scoping out the room and does the same. Two guards, one behind the counters and one in front. The counters have small handguns, the long guns are stored on shelves behind the guards.

"Good morning," the guard standing in front of the shelves says.

"Good morning," Fi says back.

"What brings you here?" The guards asks.

"Hunting party," Fi says.

"I see. She your partner?" The guard asks.

"Yes, it's her first time, so I was thinking a pistol for her," Fi says.

"People or animals?" The guard asks.

"What?" Fi asks.

"What are you hunting, people or animals?" He asks again.

Fi fills with enormous anger instantly, he does his best to contain it.

"Deer," Rose says, picking up on Fi's silence. "I really like that one," Rose says pointing in the counter at her stolen pistol. "Reminds me of my brother's."

"Ah, excellent choice," the guard says. "This one actually came in just yesterday. Real fine craftsmanship," he pulls it out and sets it aside on the counter.

Rose bought Fi enough time to refocus, "I'm digging that rifle, the one with the sling," he says pointing behind the guard.

"Ah, a great choice for deer and humans alike," the guard says, grabbing the rifle, checking the chamber, then handing it over to Fi.

Fi takes the rifle, checks the chamber himself, "She is beautiful."

"This one also just came in yesterday. These two pieces were recovered by a young couple," the guard says, making the connection just then.

Fi grins then snatches the man behind the counter with his rifle sling, twisting it around his neck pulling him over the counter.

Rose panics, and throws her pistol at the other guard, nailing him square in the face. He falls to the ground, before he can process anything, Rose is already on top of him, one quick slam of his head on the ground and he's out.

"Where's my armor?" Fi whispers to the guard he's strangling.

The guard isn't speaking, but trying desperately to make noise.

"I made the armor myself, I'm not leaving without it," Fi says, twisting the rifle more, tightening the sling.

Rose retrieves her pistol on the ground, then goes behind the counter looking for her belt with her holster. Rose looks to Fi, seeing the guards face changing colors, she remembers what Lucious said to her. She gets others to kill for her. Rose realizes what she has done. All thoughts have ceased as she thinks about how she just beat a guy unconscious without hesitation or second thought. Is this the monster from her nightmares?

"Rose, see anything back there?" Fi asks, casually strangling the life out of a man.

Now Rose sees it, sees how violent they have become. She looks back to the guard she beat down to see a blood pool around his head. She takes a deep breath, *He's not dead. I didn't kill him.* She thinks to herself. She looks back to Fi to see him break the guards neck and toss the lifeless body to the side. For a moment Rose sees Rand in place of Fi, the violence shocks her.

"These people hunt others for sport, I'm not shredding any tears," Fi says.

That's exactly what Rand would say.

"We're running out of time, do you see our armor?" Fi says, jumping over the counter.

Rose snaps out of it and gets back to looking. "Found my belt," she says, putting it on and holstering her pistol.

"Great, I'll find our armor, you look for ammo," Fi says.

"I'm not seeing any ammo here," Rose says, moving around the armory.

"I'm not seeing my armor either," Fi says.

"Fi, there's a backroom over here," Rose says, calling Fi over.

"That's got to be it," Fi says, catching up with Rose.

"It's locked," Rose says, twisting the doorknob. "Did you see a key?"

"We're running out of time," Fi says, trying to jimmy the door open.

"I'll look for the key," Rose says, going back over to the body of the guard she knocked out. She's searching his pockets when he suddenly grabs her wrist.

The half conscious man reaches for Rose with his other hand, Rose panics and slams his face into the ground again. His hands relax as a pool of blood grows beneath his head. She panics more, she doesn't know if she killed him. She can't think about this now, she runs to the other body, the one Fi killed.

Rose searches the dead man's pockets until she finally finds a key. As soon as she stands up, there's a loud crash from where Fi was. Rose runs there to see the door kicked open.

"I'm in," Fi says, looking over the door proudly.

"I just got the key," Rose says.

The sound alerts the guards outside, one walks in to see the bodies and calls for the other. As the second guard is checking on the guy Rose killed, the first guard catches Fi and Rose at the door. "Hands now!"

Fi doesn't hesitate, throwing his knife at the soldier, landing just below his collar bone. He screams out in a panic giving Fi enough time to jump to him ripping out the knife then piercing his throat with it. Blood splashes on Fi's face, he sees the guard grasping at his neck, the light draining from his eyes as he glares past Fi into emptiness.

Fi shakes, looking at the blood. Remembering his first time taking a life with his sword. Having flashbacks to that feeling.

The other guard approaches fast with his rifle up, trying to get an angle on Fi who's on the other side of the dead guard. He's yelling to Fi but he can't hear anything. His memories are too loud.

Rose quickly picks up the loaded rifle and fires a large burst at the other guard, enough shots land to drop the guard. He's not dead, but screaming in agony with shots all over his leg and up his chest. Rose looks at her handiwork, another body. Another person she killed.

The shots finally wake Fi from his trance, he looks to see the other guard dead then back to see Rose holding the rifle, staring at the body. Fi calmly takes the rifle from Rose and puts one round in the man's head, shutting him up instantly.

Rose can't even process all of her emotions right now. So much is happening.

Fi finally gets back to his old self, burying the feelings to worry about another day. He steps into the room, "Hello ammo," he says looking at tons of ammunition all around the room. He takes a deep breath and buries those emotions to focus on the here and now.

Rose isn't able to do that, she's still locked in with her emotions. Her mind froze trying to feel all those emotions all at once.

"We need to hurry," she finally manages to say, with no emotion in her voice.

"Our mags should still be here," Fi says, looking around the shelves. "Look for your pistol rounds."

"I don't see it," Rose says, her tone still emotionless.

"Me neither. My armor isn't here either," Fi says upset. There's a lot of commotion outside and Fi is still searching.

"We need to go now!" Rose says, giving in to her emotions and feeling fear over guilt.

"We can't go out there without our mags and ammo," Fi says.

"We can't stay here," Rose says, panicking. She feels alone, even with Fi there.

"Oooh, this will help," Fi says, picking up a grenade.

"You think a grenade will get us out of this?" Rose asks.

"No, but two grenades will," Fi says, picking up another one.

"How will that get us out?" Rose asks.

"Oh baby, say hello to papa," Fi says, pulling out a whole case of grenades. "You see, we arrange these around the room," Fi says, tossing grenades around the room. "Then we take this guy and tie a string to the safety pin," Fi self narrates his actions.

There's commotion outside, more people are just out of the armory, shouting about gunshots. None are coming in as none of them have weapons. "I'll get the gate guards!" one says.

Fi is still talking to himself, setting the grenades around the room. "Then we place this one behind the door with the string tied to the door," Fi says, holding the string.

"But before that, we take this other one and throw it out there," he says, pulling the pin and throwing the live grenade out of the backroom into the main armory area as people start to enter.

"Grenade!" Someone shouts, followed by an explosion.

Fi smirks, "now we throw a lot out there with the pins," he says, following his own instructions.

"What are you doing?!" Rose finally yells.

"Getting us out of here," Fi says, pulling the pin off another grenade.

"By killing everyone?!" Rose shouts.

"These people hunt others for sport. No one will care," Fi says, opening the door and tossing the grenade. "Not that these guys have any value to them anyway," he tells Rose.

"Lookout!" The entire armory except the reinforced backroom is destroyed.

"Now we tie this string to the door and escape out the back," Fi says.

Rose can't believe how fast Fi went to murder. And using Rand's own justification. She's in shock, just following him out. They escape out a window and run through an alley to the wall.

As soon as they reach the wall they hear the next explosion. A much, much bigger explosion.

Fi looks back and smiles at Rose, "There goes the rest of their armory."

Rose can't even say anything, she can't believe his actions.

Fi cups his hands together over his knee and leans down a bit, waiting to give Rose a boost over the wall.

Rose is in a daze, she can tell what is happening, but it's as if it's all in slow motion. She's processing everything slowly.

"Come on, give me foot," Fi says.

Rose steps on his hands and he boosts her up the wall. She throws one leg over to balance herself, then leans down to catch Fi.

Fi takes a running jump and grabs onto her hand. "Nice," he says, getting lifted up as he reaches to the top to pull himself up.

Fi looks back to see no one chasing them, no one's even in sight. "They don't even know where we are," Fi says smiling. "Let's keep it that way," he says, swinging his legs over the wall and dropping down.

Rose follows suit close behind.

"We should run until we're out of sight," Fi says. "Just in case."

Rose nods and they both take off running. Rose is still in denial of Fi's actions.

Heart To Heart

After a while of running, Fi finally stops, "I'm sure we're far enough now," he says, slowing to a walk. He looks to Rose who is still in deep thought. "Rose?"

No response.

"Rose," Fi says louder.

"Huh?" Rose says, snapping back to reality.

"You haven't said a word, what's up?" Fi asks.

"You killed so many people," Rose says.

"Those people hunt others for sport," Fi says. "They were the ones that shot at us."

"You killed so many," Rose says again.

"Would you rather be dead?" Fi says, frustrated. "Where is this coming from?"

"You sound like Rand used to. You're now killing because you can, not because you have to," Rose says.

"If I didn't kill them we would still be there, either dead or worse," Fi says, getting agitated.

"You made me kill," Rose says, her voice getting soft.

"What are you talking about?" Fi asks. "I shot him."

"That guard. He woke up when I was looking for the key. I tried to knock him out again, but I did it hard," Rose says, full of regret.

"If you didn't kill him he would've been in the room we were in, he would've gotten to us," Fi says.

"We weren't even supposed to be there in the first place," Rose says.

"It's not our fault we got caught," Fi says.

"We aren't supposed to be out there. We should be looking out west, not testing Lucious," Rose says.

"You are just as curious as I am. If you really didn't want to be here you wouldn't be here," Fi says.

"Lucious was right," Rose says with a sad sigh.

"What?" Fi says, sure he misheard her.

"Lucious was right," Rose repeats.

"What are you talking about? Where did that come from?" Fi says, really agitated now.

"When we talked. He said I don't kill because I have others around me that kill for me. And he was right," Rose says.

"He said that to you?" Fi asks, calming down.

"At the graveyard," Rose says.

"He's wrong," Fi says.

"No he's not," Rose disagrees, "Everyone that needed to die, needed to die to protect others, are dead."

"There's nothing wrong with that. We save people by stopping bad people," Fi says.

"By killing. We save people by killing. Where's the line?" Rose asks.

"We draw the line where we need it to be," Fi says.

"Then we are just the same," Rose says.

"No we're not. We kill to save lives," Fi says.

"If you kill a killer the number of killers are the same," Rose says.

"Damnit Rose, then we'll kill all of them," Fi says.

"Who will kill you?" Rose asks.

"I will stop anyone trying to kill me. You've got nothing to worry about," Fi shouts.

"Rand thought like that too," Rose looks into Fi's eyes, her gaze piercing his soul. "Not again," she mutters, then meeting his glare for a moment after then breaking with tears. "I can't do that again. Not to you."

Fi remembers what Rose said to him before, about not going down the same path Rand did, that she would have to stop him.

A moment passes, the air is tense.

"I couldn't stop you," he says, holding his arms out from his sides.

"I couldn't do it," Rose says, sobbing. She looks up again into his eyes, "I love you."

Fi is at a complete loss of words. He doesn't know what to feel right now, so many emotions so quickly in this argument.

Rose sees him hesitate. Maybe he doesn't feel the same. She begins thinking *I just threatened to kill him. And I told him I love him.* She feels crushed. Everything is crashing down on her.

"Rose, I've always struggled with emotions," Fi starts after his silence. "I didn't feel anything until I met you, then I started feeling everything… every moment we're together. I love you too," he finally says.

Upon hearing that, Rose's heart skips a beat, she misses a breath. She had a strong feeling Fi felt the same, the hesitancy made her doubt, but hearing it out loud. Hearing him say it made it real.

"I'm sorry I got caught up with Lucious, I'm sorry about everything" Fi adds. "Let's just go home."

Rose smiles through the tears. "Okay."

They have a long, silent, awkward walk home holding hands the whole way.

On their way home, they see a large amount of people armed approaching them blocking off their path home.

"Act natural or aggressive?" Rose asks.

"We have no ammo," Fi says.

"They don't know that," Rose says.

"They will see my rifle clearly missing a mag," Fi says.

"So what do we do?" Rose asks.

"Get off the path and let them pass," Fi says.

They both step off the path and walk alongside it, getting out of the way of the armed men.

"Rose?! Fi?!" A voice calls out from the group.

"Yeah?" Rose calls back.

The leader charges, running to get to them. As he approaches Fi and Rose recognize the man as Oscar.

"Oscar?" Rose and Fi call out together.

"We were so worried, what happened?" Oscar asks.

"We were kidnapped," Fi says. "We got out, they lost a lot of people."

"Where's your armor?" Oscar asks.

"We didn't get that back. Or ammo," Rose says, drawing her empty pistol.

"Oh, well I can fix one of those issues," Oscar says, reaching into his pockets and pulling out one rifle mag and one pistol mag from different pockets. He offers the rifle mag to Fi and the pistol mag to Rose. Then motioning for them to follow him back to his patrol.

"Thanks very much," Fi and Rose say together.

"Of course," Oscar says with a smile.

"How many are back at the base?" Fi asks.

"A few," Oscar says.

"Just a few?" Rose repeats, concerned.

"You were in trouble. I grabbed as many as I could and we came looking."

"I really appreciate this, Oscar. But we need to get back, now," Rose says.

"Yeah, you're safe, you're stocked up on ammo, let's go," Oscar says.

"Everyone, thank you for coming after us," Fi starts in a loud voice. "We're safe now, let's get back home ASAP."

"Yessir," they all say, turning around and starting their march back.

"Can you fill me in on the details?" Oscar asks.

"Now's not the time," Fi says. "Right now we need some water and run back."

"Run? Are we in trouble?" Oscar asks.

"I don't know. The ones that grabbed us, they are with Lucious," Fi says.

"They hunt people for sport," Rose adds.

"Woah, so you killed Lucious's people?" Oscar asks.

"They weren't Lucious's people, but they were allies with him," Rose says.

"How can you be sure?" Oscar asks.

"They don't look like Lucious' men, they dress very differently. But they talked about Lucious like a friend," Fi says.

"And you killed some of them?" Oscar asks.

"Yes, to escape," Fi says.

"How many?" Oscar asks.

"Not sure, but there were a lot of explosions," Rose says.

"Explosions?" Oscar repeats surprised.

"Fi found some grenades," Rose says.

Fi smiles.

"Grenades?!" Oscar says in surprise.

"Yeah, it was awesome," Fi says, causing Rose to frown.

Unnoticed, Rose shakes her head.

"How many grenades?" Oscar asks.

"A lot," Fi says back.

"Okay, that's enough! We're exposed out here, we need to get back before they find us," Rose says.

"You think they know?" Oscar asks, concerned.

"We gave them our names," Fi says, now sounding worried. "They'll probably go to Lucious about this."

"Do we strike first?" Oscar asks.

"We can't go against them," Rose growls firmly.

"If conflict is inevitable, we should take them by surprise," Fi says.

Rose clenches her fist. She has to keep control. Her gaze returns to Fi.

"Let's discuss this at home," Fi says, taking off in a sprint.

Rose looks back to the rest of the troops close behind, "Let's go!" She yells, then runs after Fi.

The Plan

Rose reaches the base just after Fi does, the gate is already open and Filip is talking to Fi.

"My lady!" Filip calls out upon seeing her walk in. "I'm so glad you're safe."

"It's good to be back," Rose says. "I trust Fi filled you in on everything?"

"Not everything, but he did cover the main things."

"We're telling everyone what happened in a meeting," Fi says.

"Okay," Rose agrees, then looks back for the rest of the troops.

Oscar arrives next, "what'd I miss?"

"Just pleasantries," Rose says. "Where's the rest?"

"Not far, they're coming," Oscar says, panting out of breath.

"You need to run more," Fi says, just fine.

"I used to run a lot, just not full sprint for that long. With all this extra weight too," Oscar says, defending himself.

"We need to gather in the command center," Rose says.

"Yeah, once our main force arrives," Fi says, looking at the gate.

Right on queue, the troops enter through the still open gate. "Sir," one says out of breath.

"Perfect, close the gate. All soldiers aside from the perimeter guards go to the command center. We need to talk," Fi shouts.

Fi holds his arm out to Rose, she pauses, but then wraps her arm around his as they lead everyone to the command center.

"First off I wanted to thank you all personally for staging that rescue op. As many know, when Rose and I were scouting for the fuel depot we were attacked by snipers. Initially we thought they came from the fuel depot," Fi starts off.

"You ran into them again?" Oscar asks.

"Yes, I'm positive it was them. They hunt people for sport," Fi says.

"Any evidence linking these guys?" Oscar asks.

"We got caught in some of their traps where they first shot at us the last time," Rose says. "Would be quite a coincidence if they weren't the same group."

"When we escaped I got a look at their armory, these are the same people," Fi says. "Anyway, there was a mention of Lucious. These guys may be allies with him. We… did kill some to escape."

"Are you saying Lucious is after us?" Oscar asks.

"We don't know," Fi says.

"Hopefully they don't know who we are," Rose says.

"Did you say anything that could lead them back to us?" Oscar asks.

"No," Rose says quickly. "Nothing said could identify us or where we are."

Fi is surprised by her immediate and blatant lie. "Regardless, there's not many that live around here," Fi says.

"So they got circumstantial proof at best?" Oscar asks.

"They'll eventually narrow it down to us. I think we should take the important stuff and leave," Fi says.

The crowd fills with gasps.

"You want us to leave?" Oscar asks.

"Sir, this place has everything," one says.

"It does. We can set up a place further out west. Gardens can be replanted, bullets can be built elsewhere," Fi says.

"Sir, are we really considering leaving?" Oscar asks.

Rose is surprised by Fi's selflessness to walk away from this completely. *He's giving up on this grudge with Lucious. He's really trying to be better,* Rose thinks with a big smile.

"Rose, do you have anything to say in this matter?" Fi asks.

"I think getting away from the fight is the best thing we can do," Rose says. "Both my parents died here, I don't want to join them. I don't want anyone else to join them either."

"Is that it?" Oscar asks.

"What do you mean?" Fi asks.

"After all this, everything we've done, we're just going to run away," Oscar says.

Fi pauses, is there a better way to word this? Is it really the right plan?

"This area isn't safe."

"We'll make it safe!" Oscar protests.

"They outnumber us, the reality is we don't have much of a chance," Fi says.

"Do you have any idea how much I've sacrificed?!" Oscar says, raising his voice. "How much we all sacrificed to be here?" the crowd shouts in agreement. "Now, we're just going to run away because they *might* come after us?!"

"Oscar," Fi says, trying not to get agitated by his outburst.

"If they're after us what's stopping them from hunting us? If we leave we'll be lost and vulnerable!" Oscar shouts. Again, the crowd chimes in agreeing loudly

"That's enough!" Fi finally shouts. "Everyone go to your quarters and cool off."

Oscar spins around and leaves without a word.

"I understand what you guys went through to get here. I don't think there's anything else we can do in this situation," Fi says.

"He's right," Rose whispers to herself.

Fi looks over at Rose thinking she's agreeing with him, but seeing her face makes him realize… She agrees with Oscar.

"You know what," Fi says to the crowd, "Let's sleep on this. Gather again tomorrow. Dismissed."

The soldiers all leave the command center in a dead silence.

Fi moves over to Rose, seeing her sad. "I thought this would be best. Is this not what you want?"

"I want this to be over with," Rose says, sitting with him.

"That doesn't answer the question. You don't want to leave, but if we stay here we'll have to deal with Lucious," Fi says.

"I know what you're doing, I appreciate it. I do," Rose says, looking up at him.

"But," Fi says, waiting for her to finish.

"But leaving would only make them chase us," Rose says.

"That's even if they can link us there," Fi says. "I killed my guy, your guy may not remember it. He was under a lot of stress."

"So why would we need to leave if they probably won't know it was us?" Rose asks.

"You don't want to leave, okay. I just thought that would be what you wanted," Fi says. "We can stay."

"I know why you thought about leaving. I understand," Rose says, grabbing Fi's hand. "This place is the first place I've felt at home with since everything… all this happened with you by my side."

At the same time, it dawns on Fi. "You're right, I was going down the path your brother did." he sees it more now, as he admits it, "I don't want that, I want to stay with you, be a man we can both be proud of," Fi says, leaning in.

"You already are," Rose says, leaning in too. They meet in the middle for a quick kiss, they close their eyes and imagine themselves anywhere but here. Any place that's more peaceful. After their lips contact they both look down leaving their foreheads touching.

Fi strategically places one hand on her shoulder and the other on her opposite cheek. This is everything he ever wanted. To fit in, to be loved. To have a place where he belongs.

Rose moves both of her hands cupping his face. She has everything she wants, to be an equal, to be loved. To have a place to call home.

"I will fight for you, for this, til the day I die," Fi says, interrupting the silence.

"I will fight by your side, for this, until the day I die," Rose says back.

They both start tipping their heads for another kiss when someone bursts into the room holding a radio.

Radio

"We have a situation!" Jeremy shouts.

The sudden urgency jolts both Fi and Rose, they both stand in a hurry.

"What is it, Jeremy?" Fi asks.

Jeremy gets up close to the duo before answering. "We have a spy."

"A spy?" Fi asks.

"The radio has been tampered with," Jeremy says.

"What do you mean tampered with?" Fi asks.

"It was set to a different frequency then we use. I didn't see who it was, they bolted once I caught them," Jeremy says.

"Do you know what frequency it was set on?" Fi asks.

"Lucious, or at least his people," Jeremy says.

Fi's and Rose's eyes enlarge, "What makes you so sure?" Rose asks.

"Who else would a spy try communicating to after you told all of us about how you killed people aligned with Lucious?" Jeremy asks.

"Coincidence isn't evidence. Definitely keep an eye out for whoever our spy could be and an ear on that radio. I want to know who's on the other end," Fi says.

"Yes sir," Jeremy says.

"Jeremy, put armed guards on the radios," Fi says. "Men you trust personally."

"Right away," Jeremy says, leaving the command center.

"I can't believe this," Fi says, "I thought we were secure."

"We should go more privately to talk," Rose says.

Rose enters her room first, looking for anything out of the ordinary.

Fi comes in right behind her, closing the door. "How are we going to do a full investigation on this?"

"Too many people. Everyone has free roam," Rose says.

"Yeah this is nothing like the capital," Fi says.

"Yeah, we don't know anything about who we're looking for," Rose agrees.

"It can't be one of ours, right?" Fi asks.

"I hope not. We brought in so many people since we last encountered Lucious. No one here likes Lucious," Rose says.

"Our people are loyal to us," Fi says. "They wouldn't jump ship just like that."

"But that's what got them here in the first place," Rose says. "What if someone's fear of Lucious is greater than their loyalty to us? Or worse, Lucious planted spies with the families we brought in."

"I don't think so. We don't have anything for either side though," Fi says.

"Wait", Rose suggests, "We're assuming the radio was used to report, what if it was used to listen in on Lucious?"

"Spying on Lucious?" Fi asks.

"We were missing for a while, plenty of time to search other radio frequencies to find us," Rose says.

"That makes sense. Like how we found Oscar leading the rescue party on the same road on the way back," Fi says, connecting the dots.

"He was the first to leave the meeting, once the meeting ended Jeremy found the radio already on that frequency," Rose adds.

"Let's go talk to Oscar," Fi says.

"Do you think he's had enough time?" Rose asks.

"He'll be fine once we tell him we aren't leaving," Fi says.

"Okay, let's go," Rose says, leading Fi out of her room and closing the door behind them.

Fi and Rose arrive at Oscar's room and knock.
"Hey Oscar, it's Fi. Wanted to talk to you," Fi says through the door.
Silence.
"Oscar I'm here too," Rose says. "Just want to talk."
Still nothing.
"Oscar? You in there?" Fi calls out, knocking again.
More silence.
Fi grabs the door knob to enter when Rose stops him.

"Don't go in there," Rose says.

"Why are you stopping me?" Fi asks, confused.

"You can't go in his room without permission," Rose says.

"If he's hiding something we should investigate," Fi says. Lowering his voice to a whisper, "if he's our spy we need to find proof."

"We don't know that yet," Rose says. "Let's look around for him."

"Alright, let's check the courtyard," Fi says.

"Then the mess hall, he may be eating," Rose says.

"Probably working off that frustration with training," Fi says.

"There he is, entering the mess hall," Rose says, pointing in a manner that Fi can't see.

"Oscar," Fi calls out, once he sees Oscar.

Oscar turns around to see Fi and Rose approaching and turns the other way.

"Why's he avoiding us?" Rose asks aloud.

"Doesn't matter, but we need to catch him," Fi says, speeding up.

"Oscar we just want to talk," Rose shouts, speeding up with Fi.

Fi and Rose finally corner Oscar.

"I just want to be left alone," Oscar says.

"Sorry we can't do that right now," Fi says.

"Oscar, we decided against moving," Rose says.

"Oh," Oscar's demeanor completely changes. "Why did you chase me all the way out here just to tell me that?"

"We have a spy," Fi whispers.

"A spy?" Oscar repeats.

"Yes. We found someone tampered with the radio. A frequency we believe to be used by Lucious," Fi says.

"It can't be one of our people," Oscar says. "It just can't be."

"At this time we aren't sure if it was used to spy for us, or spy for them," Rose says.

"What do you mean?" Oscar asks.

"We think you tampered with the radio," Fi says bluntly.

"What?" Oscar says, surprised and defensively. "What makes you think I would do that?"

"Oscar, we're not saying you're a spy for Lucious," Rose says.

"What we know is after we escaped our captors we met up with you on the path home. We know you left our meeting early after your outburst, shortly after the meeting was when we found the radio tampered with," Fi says.

"You're accusing me of reporting to Lucious? I want him dead," Oscar says aggressively.

"Like I said, we don't know at this time if the person used the radio to eavesdrop on Lucious or report to him," Rose says.

"You think I just happened to find his radio frequency?" Oscar asks. "If I found his radio frequency I wouldn't be hiding it."

Fi and Rose's eyes met in agreement.

"Thank you for your time, Oscar," Fi says.

"So is that it?" Oscar asks.

"Yeah," Fi says with a sigh. "That means we do have a spy."

"I will interview all of my troops, I will not tolerate any spies," Oscar says. "And I'll watch that radio personally."

"Once Jeremy brought this to our attention I put more soldiers guarding the radios," Fi says.

"It could be one of Jace's guys," Rose suggests.

"Probably. Which is why we can't let this get out. We'll deal with this ourselves," Fi says.

"Who all knows?" Oscar asks.

"The three of us and Jeremy," Rose says.

"Let's keep it small. The less that know about it the less chance of this getting out," Fi says.

"Wouldn't he already know we're after him? Jeremy said he caught him using the radio, he just ran away before he could identify him," Rose says.

They Know

"Fi! Rose!" Jeremy yells, running around frantically.

"Jeremy, over here," Fi calls out, waving an arm high.

"What is it?" Rose asks.

"They know!" Jeremy says, out of breath, holding the radio. "They know," he repeats.

"Who knows what?" Fi asks, concerned.

"Lucious, they know it was you two that killed their people," Jeremy says, trying to catch his breath.

Rose and Fi's eyes go wide, "The spy told them enough," Rose says.

"What do you know?" Fi asks.

"They're launching an attack," Jeremy says.

"Against us?" Fi asks.

"Yes, they're sending a lot of soldiers after us here at home base," Jeremy says.

"Looks like conflict is inevitable," Fi says, looking back to Rose.

"If they're after us we should hit them first," Rose says.

Fi is surprised by Rose's response. "You're right, they know of our firepower and manpower, we need to set an ambush to regain the advantage," Fi says.

"That's a good idea," Jeremy says. "Shall I tell the others?"

"No, no one says a word. This is a training exercise until we're in position," Fi says. "Jeremy, do we know their location?"

"I have a good idea based on what was said," Jeremy says.

"Let's get to the command center, we can map it out and plan an ambush," Fi says, running away, Jeremy follows quickly.

Rose has a bad feeling about this and stays behind. That's when she sees it, someone sneaking around the corner following Fi and Jeremy. *That's the spy!*

Rose watches the man trying to act as if he belonged while trying not to be recognized at the same time. She watches in amazement as he just casually walks along to the command center, looks around, then slips in.

Rose follows quickly and silently. She sneaks in the command center and looks around, it's dark, the lights are off except for the illumination from the map screen.

"Where's Rose?" Jeremy asks.

"I… don't know, let's focus," Fi says, pointing to the map.

Rose sneaks around the inner perimeter looking around for the spy, in the background she can hear the plan Fi and Jeremy are coming up with. If Rose can hear it, then so can the spy. Rose can't get them to stop planning without giving up her advantage on the spy.

Rose gets halfway around the room without any sign of this spy. Until she heard his breath. Rose freezes, the exhale is right in front of her. There's no movement, then another exhale. Rose uses the sound to pinpoint where the spy is and throws a hard kick in the shadow.

The spy falls forward on his face, the impact alerting Fi and Jeremy. They both turn to see the man face first on the ground.

Rose, not giving the spy a moment, jumps out of the shadow, "Here's our spy."

Fi draws his rifle and aims it at the man, "Identify yourself," he demands.

"He's one of Jace's guys," Rose says, getting a good look at him.

Fi carefully circles the intruder, muzzle locked on the man's forehead.

"You're not going to kill me," the man says confidently.

"And why's that?" Fi asks.

"Your girlfriend won't forgive you," the spy says, jumping to his feet to escape, just to be denied by Rose. She grabbed his shoulders from behind and threw him to the ground beside her.

He retaliates by kicking her knee making her fall towards him, then impacting her chest with his fist before she hits the ground.

Rose flops over out of breath with the wind knocked out of her. She manages to grab the spy's ankle, tripping him.

Seeing him hit Rose, Fi is ready to shoot.

"We need to know what he told Lucious," Jeremy shouts at Fi.

Fi removes his finger from the trigger, "Fine. But I'm kicking his ass," he says, placing his rifle on the table by Jeremy and charging at him.

The spy squares up, then steps aside at the last moment and throws Fi to the ground using his own momentum.

Rose is back on her feet, she throws a punch impacting the spys back, forcing him forward, he spins around quickly to confront Rose. She throws more punches at his face.

The spy raises his arms in a defensive stance and blocks all of Rose's swings. After blocking three hits, he grabs her wrist she's punching with and pulls her towards him delivering a powerful kick to her abdomen.

Rose falls to her hands and knees, that felt just like training with Oscar, same spot too.

Fi catches the spy from the side delivering a powerful jump kick to his ribs. The spy hits the ground rolling to his feet quickly. He squares up to Fi as Fi charges in. Fi hits fast and hard. All over, the spy is only able to block every other hit, taking hits from his abdomen up to his head. Fi is pumping with adrenaline, never slowing down, each hit impacting harder and harder.

The spy is quickly getting overwhelmed with Fi, he lunges between Fi's punches and grabs the back of his neck with both hands. Now in control of Fi's body, the spy throws in a few knees to Fi's abdomen then throws him to the ground. He turns around to look for Rose just in time to take a punch to his face from her.

Rose used her momentum to follow through as she jumped in the air throwing her whole body weight behind her fist into the spy's face.

The spy is thrown back from the force, he lands on his back. He gets to his knees and takes a moment. Rose looks back to Fi who's just getting up with a little head shake. She looks back to the spy to see him casually get to his feet and walk away from the door. Rose is tiring out, Fi's running low on adrenaline, the spy has to be getting tired of this too.

Rose approaches the spy casually, waiting for him to make the first move. Fi is coming up on Rose's left, a distance apart to keep spread out.

The spy darts around them to the table with the map and picks up Fi's rifle. Rose looks back to Fi and just now realizes he doesn't have his rifle on his back. Rose attempts to reach for her pistol.

"Ah," the spy shouts, aiming the rifle at Rose with his finger on the trigger. "You fought valiantly," he says, between quick breaths. "I honestly didn't think you two would put up quite a fight."

"Put that rifle down, I'm not done with you!" Fi shouts.

"Fi, you're tougher than I was told, but if I wanted you dead, you would be dead," the spy says.

"Is that why you're now hiding behind my gun?" Fi retorts.

"I'm just keeping you at a distance so I don't have to kill you," the spy says.

Just then, Jeremy jumps out from behind, hitting the spy in the head with the radio. His big arms lock around the spy's neck and hold him until he no longer moves.

Fi and Rose are speechless for a moment, processing what happened.

"Damn Jeremy! Great job!" Fi finally calls out.

"Thanks," Jeremy says humbly.

"You said you hated violence," Rose starts.

"I do hate violence, I'm a gentle giant," Jeremy says, looking down at the unconscious spy.

"The radio," Fi says, looking at the broken mess near the spy's body.

"Umm, it was the radio or you," Jeremy says, defending himself.

"I understand, you did well Jeremy," Fi says, looking at the pieces. "Think you could fix it?"

Jeremy kneels down and picks up the radio causing more pieces to fall out of it. "I can try," he says, looking at all the broken pieces.

"We definitely need two radios if we're going to war," Fi says.

"What's the plan now?" Rose asks.

"Why do we need a new plan?" Fi asks.

"He heard it," Rose says, pointing to the unconscious spy.

"He won't be reporting to anyone," Fi says, walking over to pick up his rifle.

"You're going to shoot him while he's out?" Rose asks.

"It's mercy. He won't feel anything," Fi says, pointing his rifle at the spy's head. "Rose, he knows our plan, he knows we know we're on to him. What are we going to do? Lock him up forever?"

Rose is thinking deeply on this. The man knows too much, he has to die, doesn't he?

"I'm sorry, Rose," Fi says, moving his finger to the trigger.

"Wait, let's hold him for now. We can deal with him after the attack. We can't kill a man out of fear," Rose says.

Fi takes a deep breath, "You're right. We'll lock him up. Jeremy, I need you to bring Oscar here discreetly."

"Right away," Jeremy says, leaving the command center in a hurry.

"Filip has the other radio, we won't know if Lucious knows of our plan, so we need someone there listening," Fi says. "Why don't you get the radio from them and bring it back here."

"I'm not leaving you," Rose says.

"I'm fine on my own," Fi says, throwing his rifle to his back and tying up the spy.

"This just feels like a bad time to be alone," Rose says, emotions spinning.

"What do you mean?" Fi asks, confused.

"I'm not leaving your side," Rose says. *Please*, she begs in her mind.

"Okay, Jeremy can get the radio from Filip when he gets back with Oscar," Fi says.

Jeremy and Oscar come running in together.

"I'm here, what's so urgent," Oscar stops talking once he sees the spy tied up on the ground not moving. "Umm, who's that?"

"This would be our spy," Fi says.

"You caught him, that was fast," Oscar says. "So what do you need me for?"

"I want you to gather some men you trust and lock him up somewhere discreet," Fi says.

"Sure, is he alive?" Oscar asks, seeing the body still motionless.

"He's alive, he's one hell of a fighter too," Fi says.

"He doesn't look so tough," Oscar says, looking at him.

"He took on me and Rose together. It wasn't until Jeremy surprised him from behind with an unbreakable headlock that we got him," Fi says.

"You? Unbreakable headlock?" Oscar says, turning to Jeremy surprised. "I thought you were a 'gentle giant'."

"I am. But he was about to kill Fi and Rose," Jeremy says. "I just stopped him."

"Kill?" Oscar asks.

"He got my rifle," Fi says.

He whistles, impressed.

"Okay, I'll keep two men watching him at all times," Oscar says, leaning over to pick up the body.

"Thank you," Fi says to Oscar, then turning to Jeremy. "Jeremy, could you bring the radio from the front gate in here please."

"Of course, should I bring the guards assigned to that radio too?" Jeremy asks.

"No, rearranging guards too much could tip off others, if there are others. You and the other guard that was watching the other radio can watch this one," Fi says.

"You got it," Jeremy says.

"We all need to be on the lookout for anyone looking around for our spy. The evidence suggests he's working alone, but we can never be too safe. We need to hit Lucious's people quickly before others start asking questions," Fi says.

Jeremy leaves to get the radio.

Oscar picks up the spy and takes him to a secure place to lock him up. He takes him to one of the recently finished new structures inside the second wall.

"So, what do we do?" Rose asks Fi.

"Part of me is saying we wait until morning before doing anything drastic, but if they're already planning an attack we need to act quickly,"

"What if there's still a chance for peace?"

"After we killed a bunch of their people?"

"They killed for sport, we defended ourselves. Fought for our lives," Rose says.

"They are already marching to war against us," Fi says.

"Do we know that for certain?" Rose asks.

"Jeremy said he intercepted radio chatter of them coming after us," Fi says.

"He didn't say anything about them coming here to fight, maybe they want to talk in person," Rose says, unconvincingly even to herself.

"You don't even believe that." Fi says, look her in the eyes.

"I just don't want anyone to have to die," her voice cracking .

"Yeah, me neither," Fi says with a sigh.

"I don't think I can fight with the little sleep I'm running on anyway," Rose says.

"Yeah, I'm starting to feel that too. That fight with the spy definitely took my last bit of energy," Fi says.

"Fi! Rose!" Jeremy comes running in with the radio in his arms with the other guard at the door. "Guys, the attack got called off!" He says, once he's at the table with Fi and Rose.

Rose smiles at the good news, but Fi is skeptical.

"Why?" Fi asks.

"Aren't you glad? We're not in danger tonight," Jeremy says.

"Are they onto us?" Fi asks.

"They said they didn't hear anything from their spy so they're calling off the attack, at least for now it seems," Jeremy says.

Now Rose looks concerned, "You think they know we're onto them?"

"Maybe they were waiting for their spy to tell them if we were going to intercept them, without word from their spy they won't attack," Fi says.

Now Jeremy is concerned, "So the longer we hold the spy, the safer we are or the more danger we're in?"

"It seems both," Fi says. "We need to find the sweet spot in the middle."

"Next move?" Rose asks.

"I need to sleep on this," Fi says. "Jeremy, I want you on that radio at all times. In fact, Oscar and you can both watch over the prisoner and radio together with the added guards he has."

"Do we want the radio to be with the prisoner?" Jeremy asks.

"He's not getting out unless we let him out. Don't let him out," Fi says. "He doesn't need to be in earshot of the radio."

"Yes sir," Jeremy says, picking up the radio to head out.

"Jeremy, tell Oscar he's in charge. If he needs anything, wake me," Fi says.

"And me," Rose says, interjecting.

"Of course," Jeremy says, heading out.

"Looks like we get our rest," Fi says, letting out a big yawn.

"About time," Rose says, returning with a yawn.

"Well good night," Rose says.

"Walk you to your room?" Fi says, holding out his arm.

"Sure," Rose says, wrapping her arm around his.

Rose lays down dressed with her gun belt to be ready at a moment's notice. Now that she's thinking about sleep she feels incredibly tired. She's out as soon as her head hits the pillow.

Once More

Rose wakes to the sound of their big guns firing. The sound startles her and she falls out of bed. She rushes to her feet and out the door to the balcony for an advantage.

She gets there to see soldiers along the balcony shooting out into the distance. She draws her pistol but can't seem to see attackers. Everyone is joining in the fight, even Jace's troops and others that joined them. Rose's pistol doesn't have the range to shoot from up here, she sees Fi on the gate and starts running down the stairs.

"Fi!" Rose calls out, at the base of the wall. "What's going on?"

"They tried to catch us sleeping, jokes on them," Fi says right at the big guns fire again.

"Is it Lucious?" Rose shouts back.

"I don't know," Fi shouts in return. "No one's gotten close enough to identify."

After another barrage from the big guns everything falls silent.

"Oscar, take your scouts and check for survivors. Bring any here," Fi shouts.

"On it!" Oscar calls back, climbing off the wall.

"Opening the gate!" Filip calls out, opening the gate.

Several troops run out after Oscar, leaving the rest on the wall watching over the scouts.

"That's it?" Rose asks, walking next to Fi.

"That's it," Fi confirms.

"I was expecting a lot more," Rose says.

"We have big guns," Fi says, gesturing to the canons. "And the high ground. It was never going to be a long battle."

"Did we lose anyone?" Rose asks.

"None that I've seen," Fi says, looking around the wall and courtyard. "Ah, just in time," Fi says, as the scouts return to the wall with a dozen prisoners. They all have their hands on their heads walking in a line.

"All the survivors," Oscar says, lining them up outside the wall.

"Wonderful. Any sign of Lucious?" Fi calls down.

"None sir," Oscar reports.

Fi climbs down the stairs exiting the gate to face the prisoners. "Well that's bad news for you," he says, to the prisoners.

"I'm not saying a word," one says.

"I know," Fi says calmly. "In fact, that will be your last word," he says, as he deliberately raises his gun and shoots the man in the face.

Rose is frozen in shock for a moment until she heads down to Fi.

"Are you going to talk?" Fi asks, aiming his rifle at the next prisoner in line.

"Go to hell," the prisoner says.

"Prepare my throne," Fi snarls, shooting him in the head.

"Fi! What are you doing?!" Rude yells, grabbing his rifle and forcing the muzzle down.

"I want Lucious. These people don't matter," Fi says to Rose, then looking back to the next prisoner in line. "Where's Lucious?"

"You best listen to your girlfriend," another prisoner says.

Fi flicks his rifle up quickly to shoot the man, Rose tries to stop it, but Fi still lands a round in the center of the man's chest. He falls over screaming in pain for a moment before the shock sets in and he bleeds out.

"Next!" Fi calls out, side stepping to the next prisoner.

Rose takes the opportunity and shoves Fi to the ground, standing over him with her pistol pressed firmly against his chest. "No! Stop it!" she cries.

"These people kill for sport, I'm not shedding any tears," Fi says. "Once I kill Lucious it'll be over."

Rose disengages the safety on her pistol, "It's over now. We won."

"As long as Lucious is alive, we are in danger. These men came after us cause we killed some in self defense, we just killed more in self defense. A lot more. What do you think he'll do next?" Fi asks.

"Rose, get off him," Oscar says gently, eyeing the prisoners nervously.

"Oscar, do me a favor and shoot the next one in line," Fi says bloodthirsty.

"Don't do it Oscar," Rose says, not moving her eyes from Fi.

"Rose, I love you, but you live in a fantasy. Out here it's kill or be killed, and I don't want you to be killed," Fi says.

"No it's not! We made peace once before, we can make peace again!" Rose shouts.

"You're insufferably naive sometimes," Fi says, moving to get up.

"Uh-uh," Rose says, pulling the hammer back on her pistol.

"What? Are you really going to shoot me? For protecting you?" Fi says.

"I don't need you protecting me!" Rose shouts with her finger on the trigger.

"If it wasn't for me protecting you, you and Rand would've both died at the capital. You would've died at the targeting facility. You need others to protect you, you're nothing on your own-,"

Rose pulls the trigger through her tears.

This was it. She actually did it. Just like when she put Rand down when he lost his way. Fi lost everything, his humanity, his grace, he's a killer. Everything Rose loved about him was gone. And now so was he. She watched the light fade from his eyes. He doesn't even look surprised or angry. He knew this was coming.

Rose crawls back from Fi dropping her pistol and letting out a loud scream. After she screams she rubs her eyes, once she opens them again she sees Fi standing in front of her with a smile.

"Damn," Fi says, looking at the hole in his chest. "I knew you had it in you. Right in the heart too. You didn't even give your brother that kind of mercy."

Rose looks around to see everyone applauding her. The dead men around are now standing and clapping.

"You just killed the one person you have left. Great job," Oscar says.

"You murdered the two people you have loved the most in your life. Well done indeed," Fi says.

Upon hearing that Rose thinks of her brother too, her conscience makes him appear before her. Laying on the ground with a knife sticking out of his gut, looking up at Rose. She can't believe what's going on. Finally she realizes she's dreaming again, upon that realization she wakes up covered in sweat.

Late Night Chat

"What is wrong with me?!" Rose says out loud. "Is this who I am?"

She realizes her pillow is soaked with tears and sweat, so she climbs out of bed. It's the dead of night.

"Fi's right, we need to end this threat. I'm done being naive."

Rose leaves her room quietly to not disturb others. She sneaks to Fi's room and knocks gently. "Fi, you awake?" She whispers.

There's movement beyond the door, then the door opens.

"Rose? Can't sleep either?" Fi says.

"Another nightmare, um, actually," Rose says, looking into Fi's eyes.

"So, what can I do?" Fi says nervously.

"Can we talk?" Rose asks.

"Of course," Fi says, opening the door more, "Come in."

"Thank you," Rose says, walking in and looking for a place to sit.

"So, what do you want to talk about?" Fi asks.

"That first nightmare I told you about, do you remember it?" Rose asks, sitting on the corner of his bed.

"Yeah, pretty well," Fi says.

"I've had the same dream over and over again with different people," Rose says. "It feels so real. I feel those people die."

"I'm right here now, I'm not going anywhere," Fi says, sitting next to her with his hand on her shoulder.

"You didn't just die this time," Rose says, her eyes starting to water.

"Did I do something bad? Something worse than just dying?" Fi asks.

"Lucious sent people to attack us, we won. You started interrogating the prisoners and executing them," Rose says.

"Woah, I would never kill unarmed people, especially prisoners," Fi says.

"I know, you wouldn't. But in this nightmare you did. I had to put you down," Rose says, now letting the tears flow.

"Oh. I understand what you're feeling now," Fi breathes deep. "You didn't just watch me die this time... you... killed me."

"I just need to hold onto you for a while," Rose says, hugging him.

"Of course, I always welcome hugs," Fi says, with a smile.

After what feels like an eternity of embracing one another Rose breaks the quiet, "You were right. You were always right."

"Is this coming from your dream?" Fi asks.

"I finally get it. Lucious is a threat to us. As long as he's alive we're in danger," Rose says.

"Hey, you can't take my side, I finally accepted your side," Fi says, half joking.

"I don't think we can have peace, not after what we did," Rose says.

"What I did," Fi clarifies.

"I was there too. I wanted to go out there too," Rose says, finally accepting her part of the blame.

"Wow, that dream really changed you," Fi says.

"I don't want to live in fear," Rose says.

"You've seen our walls and our guns, we don't need to fear anything," Fi says.

"He has way more people, our guns won't matter if there's no one to use them," Rose argues.

"Do you want a frontal charge at Lucious's base?" Fi asks. "We don't know exactly where he is, and the last time we went out that direction we -."

"I know. We need to ambush them. Lucious is a prideful man, he would definitely be leading his assault, we just need to ambush him. Our big guns can wipe them out before he even gets closer enough to attack," Rose suggests.

"I let that hate go, you need to let your fear go," Fi says.

"I can't, please," Rose begs.

Fi sighs. "There's no going back after this. All of his allies, all of his people will come after us."

"We'll take care of them too."

Fi, don't we deserve a happy life together?"

"We'll talk it over in the morning with our troops," Fi says.

"I don't know where this is coming from, I don't know if I'm still dreaming, but this needs to end. I don't care, he needs to die. I don't care how many need to die to kill him," Rose says.

"You must be sleep walking, there's no way my Rose would say that," Fi says, half confused and half surprised by Rose's sudden change of heart. "Why don't you go back to sleep, we'll talk about this in the morning."

"I just need to say this before I fully wake up," Rose says. "You were right."

There's a knock at the door.

"Who is it?" Fi calls out, standing up.

"Oscar, we have to talk, it's urgent," Oscar says through the door.

Fi gets to the door and opens it, "What's urgent?"

"Not out here," Oscar whispers.

Fi opens the door more for Oscar to come in then leans out and checks the hall for anyone.

"Oh, hope I'm not interrupting anything," Oscar says, seeing Rose sitting on the bed.

"We're just talking," Rose says.

Oscar looks at her eyes then to Fi's eyes, "Can't sleep?" He asks, seeing them both tired but awake.

"Bad dream," Rose says.

"I've been really stressed out lately," Fi says.

"Okay, well we intercepted communications from Lucious, he's launching an assault right now," Oscar says.

"How much time do we have?" Fi asks.

"A few hours at the most. Based on their radio chatter I've been able to narrow down where he may be coming from," Oscar says.

Fi gets up excitedly, "we know his route?"

"Roughly, I marked it on the map," Oscar says. "It lines up on the current plan to ambush him."

"This is it," Rose says. "We can finally end this threat."

Oscar looks at Rose, "I wasn't expecting that from you."

"That's what we were talking about," Fi says. "She's done living in fear and ready to take action to end this threat."

"Then let's go," Oscar says. "The previous plan is still in full effect. The ambush will work."

"Tell our troops, tell Jace's men it's a nightly exercise, they will accompany us at the front while the overwatch team comes in behind with the big guns," Fi says.

"On it, I'll get everyone ready," Oscar says, opening the door.

"Ten minutes and we're marching out here to our ambush spot," Fi says, going to the corner of his room to a dresser.

"Right on, we'll meet in the courtyard," Oscar says, heading out, closing the door behind him.

Rose turns back to Fi for any last words before she heads out.

"I'm about to change, do you mind?" Fi says, gesturing to the door.

"Yeah, I uh, I'll meet you at the courtyard," Rose says, heading out. *Is this what I want to wear when we take down Lucious?* She thinks to herself, looking down at her outfit. She heads back to her room for a different coat.

Upon entering her room, Rose goes to her closet and pulls out a nice white long coat that goes the length of her knees and has big pockets. "Ah mother, your style will definitely live on," she says to herself putting on the coat.

She then meets up with everyone at the courtyard where Fi is already up front giving orders. She missed some of it, but remembers enough from when they first planned it. She grabs a rifle on her way out. They're taking all the soldiers but the gate guards and two protecting the prisoner. No one told the civilians about this incursion, only the soldiers know.

Ambush

They march off to war. Their plan is set, by morning they will be free of fear. Rose marches up front with Fi, Oscar, and Jace's people.

They arrive at the ambush spot they planned and wait. And wait. There's no sign of Lucious's forces.

Fi begins to panic. "Oscar, you said this was the path that would take," Fi says, bringing Oscar close to him and Rose.

"This is the path that was said on the radio," Oscar responds, starting to panic.

"Did we pass by them?" Rose asks, confused.

"If we did, our home is completely undefended," Fi says.

"We only left people to guard the spy," Oscar says. "We need to get back now."

"We need to be there now," Fi agrees.

"Well Jace's troops here still think it's just an exercise, so we can head straight back now," Rose says.

"Right, okay," Fi says, standing up to face his troops.

There's some leaves rustling on their flank, before Fi can turn to look, a dozen armed men come out on their left flank. By the time Fi and the others can react, a dozen more armed men come out from their right flank.

"Fancy seeing you here," Lucious says, stepping out of the shadows.

The voice sends shivers down Rose's spine. She didn't fear him before, but now she's terrified.

"Lucious," Fi says, with a heavy sigh.

"Fi, how predictable. And you brought the little Rose with you," Lucious says.

"Go to Hell," Rose snaps back.

"I'll tell your parents you said that when I see them there," Lucious says with a grin.

"You little -," Rose raises her rifle but stops seeing many guns trained on her.

"I didn't want this to end like this. We had a deal, we had peace," Lucious says. "I like you, I really do. But it's one thing to stand up to me with peace talks, but conspiring against me with my own men?"

"This doesn't have to end violently," Rose says, trying to hide her change of heart to save the lives of her people.

"This absolutely does. You see, you killed some of my people, so I was sending my people to kill some of your people for killing my people. And then you sent out to kill more of my people. Not cool," Lucious says.

"Well unfortunately for you," Fi starts, "the leaders here are both kids. You don't kill kids."

"Conspiracy to commit murder on a grand scale, now that's a serious charge," Lucious says. "Since you two are the heart and soul of everyone here, I'm going to try you as adults."

"So you're going to kill kids and leave?" Rose mocks, "real big of you."

"Is this going to be a trial by combat, or are you still afraid?" Fi mocks.

"Fear is why you're here. Not me," Lucious says.

"We're not afraid of you," Fi growls.

"Oh yes you are. Like I told little Rose here, fear controls people far better than respect," Lucious states.

"You brought an army to face us, obviously you're afraid of us," Fi shouts.

"I was never afraid of you," Lucious starts. "I underestimated you once. You've lost your honorable death when you murdered my people."

"You never had honor," Fi says.

"Regardless, I see you brought an army to face me," Lucious says, standing before them.

"Lucious, your men trapped us and gave us no way out," Fi says, keeping his rifle at a low ready.

"You killed almost two dozen men," Lucious says.

"It was them or us," Rose says.

"Us? Little Rose, did you kill some of my men?" Lucious asks.

"I did," Rose says, feeling the guilt from accidentally killing the man.

"She killed one, I killed the rest," Fi says, tightening his grip on his rifle.

"That I can't excuse," Lucious says, sternly. "We had peace, we set up boundaries, hell I didn't even kill any of you. Then you trespass and kill my people."

"We still have more firepower here, we can renegotiate," Fi says.

"Now why would I want to negotiate with the likes of you? Especially since you brought me my reinforcements."

Then, in a moment of unbelievable horror, all of Jace's people turn their weapons on Rose and her people.

"Wait, what?" Rose says confused.

"What are you guys doing?" Fi yells, pointing his weapon at the lot of traitors. He can't pick a target, until he swings his rifle back to Lucious.

"You guys said you wanted peace, why are you turning on us?!" Rose shouts.

"Peace?" Jace's man scoffs, "you only befriended us for war."

"We befriended you to overthrow a dictator that would enslave everyone!" Rose shouts back. "We had a plan that no one would get hurt!"

"Well Lucious had a better plan. A plan where we get power," Jace's man says. "Now drop your weapons, all of them."

"I'd do what he says," Lucious says, "and get on your knees of course."

Fi, being overwhelmed with anger freezes with his rifle steadied on Lucious. All that anger for Lucious he left behind comes back.

Rose looks around, seeing they now are severely out matched, she gives in. *This is the only way my people can live.* "Do- Do as he says," Rose says, dropping her rifle.

Others begin to drop their weapons and get on their knees.

"Are you sure?" Oscar calls back. "No! Arm yourselves!"

"It's over Oscar," Rose calls back. "No one has to die today. The plan was for no one dying," Rose says.

The remaining troops drop their weapons. Only Fi and Oscar remain armed.

"Fi, do you want to be made an example again? This time in front of everyone? Drop your weapon now," Lucious says.

Fi's finger twitches on the trigger. He's all ready to pull the trigger, then looks back to Rose. Her widened eyes peered into his soul. He takes a deep breath and drops his rifle.

Oscar follows suit after Fi.

Rose is relieved, she knew nothing she could say would convince him out of it. She was ready for him to pull the trigger.

Lucious walks over to Fi, "You made the right choice," he says, pushing him to the ground. "Now kneel." He walks past to Rose, "Ah, my sweet Rose. Thank you for at least seeing reason here. But I'm going to need your pistol too," he says, holding his hand out in front of her.

Rose looks up to him, then focuses on his hand without a word.

"Rose, I won't ask again," Lucious says.

"It's my brother's pistol," she says, drawing it slowly from her holster. "It was passed down from my father."

"That only makes me want it more," Lucious says, taking it. Lucious rounds up Rose's people, keeping Rose, Fi and Oscar close. "Restrain them," Lucious says to his men, as they tie the wrists of their defeated foes.

Lucious stands over his defeated prey. Everyone on their knees, bound by their wrists. His soldiers surrounding them.

"Rose, your brother had such conviction. So much I hoped would shine onto you, but instead you just lived in his shadow," Lucious says.

"You don't know me! Or my brother! Stop pretending you do!" Rose yells back.

"He keeps bringing up Rand because he's afraid of him," Fi says. "If Rand were here, Lucious would be the one being executed."

"After doing what you knew to be right and slaying your own brother, you crawled under another shadow. A shadow of a person who will only ever be a fraction of the man Rand was," Lucious says. "Shame. You had all the potential, all the experience, but were too afraid to stand for your own."

"Without your big scary army you're nothing. You just enjoy murder and need an army to cover you so better people don't kill you first," Fi says.

"I hate to do this. People are a valuable resource. I hate wasting resources. But you two inspire too much hope and resistance. I can't have that. With your deaths, your people will fall in line quicker," Lucious says, pointing Rose' pistol. "Fi, I'm sorry to make an example out of you again."

"You're not sorry, you're just afraid of strong people, terrified of stronger people than you!" Fi shouts.

"I'm afraid of an uprising that would require me to kill more people. Two to save the many," Lucious says, lowering his gun to the back of Fi's head.

"Do it you coward!" Fi yells until he feels the muzzle press against his head. "Rose! Run!" He shouts, swinging his head back, pushing past the pistol and slamming his skull into Lucious's thigh.

Rose gets up and runs. She hears others running behind her along with gunshots. She tries her best to duck and weave. She looks back to see some others right on her trail, with their arms behind their backs too. These were her people! Her soldiers followed her! There's still hope! She glances past them to their pursuers, just in time to watch Lucious shoot Fi in the head. Tears fill her eyes, she can't believe this actually happened. Through the tears, she sees more shots kicking up dirt around her. She watches as more of her people get shot from behind. There's nothing she can do but run.

"Don't look back!" Someone shouts close behind. "Don't look ahh!"

Rose knows he was shot, she doesn't have the courage to turn around. Don't look back. The words echo in her mind. She runs until she can no longer hear gunfire. Then the adrenaline ends and she falls face first into the dirt, arms still tired behind her.

"I think we're safe," a familiar voice says in between short breaths.

Rose rolls around to see maybe a dozen people with her. She can't bear to look any of them in the eye. She wanted to face Lucious. She gave into her fear. Her fear got everyone killed. Got Fi killed.

"Okay, we need to regroup at Home Base. Regroup and rearm. Meet up with everyone there," Oscar says, removing his restraints by rubbing them on rough bark from a nearby tree.

Rose doesn't say a word. She's hoping this was all a dream.

"Rose, let me help you with your restraints," he says, walking over to her. She's completely out of it, she doesn't notice him approaching her. He grabs her arm to remove her restraints, the touch snaps her back to reality.

"Don't touch me!" Rose yells, frantically moving away.

"Woah, Rose, I'm trying to help," he says.

"Fi is dead," Rose whispers to herself. Finally coming to terms with it. "Fi is dead and his killer will pay!"

"Yes he will!" Oscar says, freeing the others. "Can I help you now?" He asks.

"Yes. Please," Rose says, turning around and holding her arms out to him. "Sorry I -."

"It's fine. That was tragic. But we have to keep going. Focus on revenge. If we lose focus we lose the war."

"You're right. Who are you?" Rose asks.

"Oscar," Oscar responds confused, "Did you hit your head?"

"Oscar, I knew that. Everything's spinning," Rose says.

"I understand, what are your orders?" He asks.

"I-I don't know," Rose says.

"You don't know? Rose, we have to kill them! We can go back to Home Base to meet up with the rest of our forces and get more weapons then get back in this fight," Oscar says.

"I don't know if I can lead," Rose says, unable to hold back the tears from what happened. "I got so many people killed."

"Your plan was well thought out, Lucious just had more people. It isn't your fault. We need you," Oscar says, trying to comfort her.

"I can't lead. Not anymore. Fi did all the planning."

"We need your leadership. Without you, the rest of us will die," Oscar says.

"We can't fight anymore," Rose says.

Oscar stands up and takes a deep breath, "My lady, if we give up now their deaths would be for nothing."

"If we die, our deaths will be for nothing," Rose snaps back.

"Fi died to save us so we could avenge him," Oscar says, raising his voice.

"Guys, not a good place to be arguing, let's get back home and talk there," one soldier says.

"Right," Rose says, "Let's get back -," her mind wanders again. She can't focus.

"We're going home," Oscar says loud enough for everyone to hear, "we're going to rearm and hit Lucious at his home. He'll never see it coming."

"That's not -" Rose doesn't have the focus to argue right now, she follows her people back to her home in deep thought. Is this fight even winnable? Should she have just given up when she was offered? Fi would still be alive. Rose follows while Oscar leads all the survivors back home.

"Open the gate!" Oscar shouts, as soon as they get within shouting distance of the front gate.

Silence.

"Open the gate!" Oscar shouts again, at the gate. "Filip!"

No response.

"Help me open this," Oscar says to the survivors.

They get the gate open enough to enter when a man with a knife lunges out at Oscar. Oscar is surprised but ready, catching the man by the wrist and shoulder he throws him passed to the ground.

Oscar draws a pistol, identifying the man as the spy they locked up. There's blood still dripping from his knife.

"Should've left more than -," the spy gets interrupted by Oscar blowing his head up with a well placed round.

"Check for -," Oscar sees Filip's body covered in blood on the ground behind the gate, looking like he was stabbed and pushed from the wall.

"Filip!" Rose calls out, rushing to his side. He's dead.

This Is Bad

"We need to rally the remaining troops and hit Lucious's base as hard as we can, as fast as we can!" Oscar says.

"Oscar, they're dead. They're all dead," Rose says in tears. "Not just the men, but the women and children too."

Finally feeling the weight Oscar says, "We just, we just have to keep going."

"Oscar, are you sure that's the best idea right now?" Someone asks.

"They were expecting us. So we have to be unpredictable. We're going to hit them head on with everything we got! It's unpredictable, that's what we need," Oscar says, waiting for the remainder of the troops to arm up for an assault.

Rose finally finds the right words, "we shouldn't risk everyone in an open assault," she says, placing her hand on Oscar's shoulder.

"That's all we can do now," Oscar says.

"I really don't think that will work. We will lose everyone else," Rose says.

"You're making Fi's death worthless!" He shouts, pulling her hand from his shoulder. "I know what I'm doing," Oscar looks around to the remaining soldiers around him, "Rand trusted me to lead, he made me captain. I'm asking you to trust me now."

"We're with you Captain," a soldier says as they all finish arming up.

"Don't let your fear -," Rose starts but gets cut off.

"If we want a shot at taking down Lucious, we need everyone we have, they're still recovering from their ambush," Oscar says. He hands a rifle to Rose but she doesn't accept it. "Are you coming?" He asks. "You're the one Fi died to protect. If you don't go, his sacrifice was for nothing."

Rose stares at the weapon as she processes what Oscar said. *You're the reason Fi died. You're the one he died to protect.* She reaches for the rifle, the weapon she desperately wants to kill with. Her pain is now bouncing between anger and revenge. She hates that feeling. She sees the weapon as just the means of killing. She Knows she can't walk down that path. She freezes with the rifle just out of her grasp.

"Fine, I'm not a fan of child soldiers anyway. Just thought you'd want to avenge Fi's death," Oscar says, pulling the rifle back.

Rose lets out a silent gasp, as what Oscar said hit deep. Everything he has said since the ambush was manipulation. Her emotions are all over the place. She can feel herself being manipulated by Oscar, she's trying hard not to give in, but in her vulnerable state all she wants is to kill.

"Okay, I don't know what you're going to do, but we're going to avenge our fallen. Avenge Fi," Oscar says.

"I can't be alone again," she says, noticing everyone is with Oscar. He turned everyone against her. "I will go with you," Rose says, feeling defeated. "I need to get something from my room first."

"Good," Oscar says, "make Fi proud."

"I can't be alone again," Rose repeats to herself.

"I understand not wanting to be alone," Oscar starts. "You have lost everyone you care about. It's time for revenge."

Rose is starting to give in to that fear, the same fear that is now controlling Oscar and her remaining people.

"Oh, I got this back for you," Oscar says, pulling her pistol out of his waistband and holding it out to her.

Rose stares at it, this weapon is different, this one was used to protect people as much as it was used to kill. This is her last memory of her brother. She reaches out and grabs it from him. Now staring at it in her hands, she knows what she has to do, but is unsure if she has the strength to do it. She plants it firmly in her holster, then starts to walk across the field to the living quarters.

"Rose!" Oscar shouts, "Where are you going?"

"Getting my brother's sword," she replies, not even turning to face him. Her voice was so low he could barely hear her.

"We don't have time for that, we gotta hit Lucious now!" Oscar shouts back as Rose slowly walks away.

"I'm not going without my brother's sword," Rose says.

"Is that really your priority right now?" Oscar continues to shout.

"It's all I have left!" Rose shouts, turning around to face Oscar.

"We're leaving now! Join us or be left behind!" Oscar shouts once more.

Rose pauses in the field. *What good would a sword do in a gun fight anyway?* She looks down and grips her pistol in her holster, *this is enough.* She turns back and walks back to Oscar and her troops.

"Lets move out! Straight to Lucious' compound!" Oscar calls out.

Rose follows behind, she doesn't have the willpower to run. She looks back at her home for what seems like the last time. She watches as they charge out of view and wonders if they're actually ready for a fight. Or if they even know where they're going. She remembers the vague area Lucious pointed to on a map during his last visit. She heads there and hopes everyone makes it there too.

Eventually she can hear gunshots. She runs towards the sound. Then all goes quiet. She stops in her tracks in fear of the outcome of the battle. She starts to panic and continues moving towards the direction she heard the shots slowly.

She finally arrives on the outskirts of Lucious' base hiding in the treeline. She looks out to see a pair of men dragging bodies away from the front of the base. Her face goes pale as she realizes what's going on. No survivors. Everyone is dead. She falls to her knees in tears. Losing Fi was horrible, but losing everyone else hurt even more. *This is my fault. I didn't have a plan. I let Oscar run that suicide mission.*

That's when she notices where they're piling the bodies, on carts. She follows as they move the cart away from Lucious' base. All that guilt turns to rage, that pain into anger. She's ready to avenge everyone she knew. Focusing on that rage, driving the sadness away, she pushes through stalking the cart.

The cart stops not too far away, but it is out of sight of the compound. She watches in bewilderment to see Lucious and others digging graves for her people. *Those are my people, right?* She recognizes the bodies that are being lifted out of the cart and set in graves. *They are burying my dead. But why?* Rose is confused.

They're mocking my people! He has to die! For Fi! She thinks to herself. Fi was upset when she didn't finish Lucious when she had the chance, now Fi's dead. If she just killed lucious then and there everyone would be alive. She draws her pistol and aims for Lucious' head. She struggles to get a clear shot, he's moving too much. *I can't get any closer, there's still too many.* She decides to wait for the other two to leave and hope Lucious stays alone.

Shadow

As the sun begins to rise the three men finish up burying all the dead. Rose can't hear what they're saying, but their body language suggests they're leaving. The two that arrived with the cart move towards the cart while Lucious remains. *This is perfect. Exactly what I need.* Rose takes aim with her pistol once more, he's kneeling down by a grave, easy pickings. Resting the sight on his head, she disengages the safety, and pulls the hammer back. *One clean shot is all I need.* She hesitates. She doesn't know why, this doesn't feel right. *I need him to know who it is that killed him. I need to be the last thing he sees.*

Rose moves closer quietly with her pistol still trained on his head. Any sudden move and she'll just blast him. The others leave with the cart, most likely heading back to their base. She manages to get up right behind Lucious, pointing the barrel directly into the back of his head.

He stands up, unaware what's right behind him.

"Killing them wasn't enough, you mock them too?" Rose says angrily, startling Lucious.

Lucious turns around in complete surprise looking down a gun barrel. "Gonna be honest, I did not see that coming," he says.

"Why?" Rose says.

"You're a lot braver than I thought," he says. "After you sent everyone to charge my base I had thought you used that distraction to disappear."

"I didn't do that," Rose denies.

"Well they all charged in blindly. I was expecting you to come after me for revenge, but I didn't expect them to just rush in without a plan," Lucious says. "You really should've had some kind of plan, I'm disappointed."

"I didn't tell them to attack!" Rose says, raising her voice.

Lucious smirks, "So their fear of me was stronger than their respect for you."

"That's not -," Rose remembers when Lucious said that to her for the first time.

"Like I said, fear controls people better than respect," he says, turning that smirk to a grin.

Realizing he's right again, she quickly tries to deflect, "Why are you mocking my people? You've already killed them," Rose demands.

"Human life is precious," Lucious says.

"Is that why you killed everyone I know?" Rose says, angrily.

"I killed them because if I didn't, a lot more people would die. A lot more blood on my hands. I'm sorry I killed everyone you knew, but I don't regret it. They left me no choice, I did what I know to be right."

"Right?! You think it was right murdering defenseless people?!" Rose yells, her anger boiling.

"If I didn't, if I let them go, a lot more of my people would be dead. Without us as guidance rebuilding civilization, more would die. That confrontation was a massive setback that will probably get more people killed. People that wouldn't be dead if we weren't fighting each other," Lucious says.

"You started this war! You started the killing! How dare you pretend to care about people when all you do is kill and enslave!" Rose shouts. "You killed Fi," Rose says, in an almost whisper. "You killed Fi. You have to die," she says, as her hands begin to shake.

"You do what you think is right," Lucious says, not moving.

"You killed Fi," Rose repeats, feeling the weight of her defeat all over again. Tears forming in her eyes, seeing her prey defenseless not even trying to fight back depletes her rage causing it to turn back to sadness. Her hands shaking too much to keep focused on her target.

"I understand," Lucious says, grabbing the muzzle and holding it still aimed at his head. "You do what you feel is right. That's all anyone can do," he says in a calm voice.

Rose looks him in the eyes and sees Rand. His words echo in her mind. Lucious is no different than Rand. Doing what he thinks is right. *Never take a life out of emotion. This is what he wants.* She lowers her gun to her side, looking down, she lets the tears go.

"I don't know what you see, but you are throwing away the last thing you have," Lucious says, sympathetically.

"I don't have anything," Rose says.

"You have vengeance. Maybe this will help," he says, pulling a small pistol from under his jacket pointing it at Rose.

"You'd really do that?" At this point Rose isn't even afraid anymore. She's just done.

"It has to end like this. We can't go our separate ways. Not after this. One of us dies here," he says firmly.

Rose doesn't even look at him, she drops Rand's pistol and falls to her knees. Knowing she's keeping the person she has worked so hard to become stops the tears.

"You're making Fi's death mean nothing. He sacrificed himself to save you, just for you to die the same way. The only thing his sacrifice did was get all your people killed. It only had to be you two. Such a shame," Lucious says, pulling the hammer back on his pistol, "I thought you had the conviction to finish this."

Rose is visibly confused.

"I heard the stories of your family. Your father; Havoc, your mother; Helen, your brother; Rand. I know all about what your brother did, he was legendary. Once I heard you killed him, I had a lot of respect for you. You stood up for what you knew to be right even to the point of killing your own brother. Turns out you're just a raging little mess of a girl."

Rose starts taking short deep breaths, the rage building up again. She looks up to see his finger on the trigger. She looks past to see Lucious, the killer of her people. Those last words were his final mistake. She moves lightning fast, grabbing his gun maneuvering her finger behind the trigger and gripping the frame with the other hand, she snaps it away before he has time to react. Then, while he's still processing what happened, she hits him in the face with the gun. The shock and impact knocked him down. She continues to use his pistol as a hammer on his face, wailing away. She stops just short of killing him, looking at the bloody mess of what once was his face, she remembers who she is. *Rose, daughter of Havoc and Helen; The Legends, Sister to Rand; The Brave.*

"Finish it!" Lucious says, barely able to speak.

"It's over," she says, dropping his gun and turning away to pick up hers.

"You're weak!" He says between coughs while gurgling blood. "Years living in your family's shadow, you can't even finish your enemies! This is why *everyone you love is dead.*"

"I cast my own shadow of the person I've become. This is who I am. Who I've become. And that's how I'll take down everything you built. Myself! I don't need anyone! I cast my own shadow, and soon that shadow will cover your once great empire!" Rose says, taking aim at Lucious with *her* pistol. "I'll start with putting you down like a dog!"

Lucious' mouth opens to speak again, but–

Her finger squeezes the trigger. The shot goes off, quieter than usual, she thinks. The damage from the shot is clear:

Lucious is dead.

She looks. Time has stopped. She waits for him to move again.

He doesn't.

Rose rises slowly and walks over to the memorial and kneels down to pay her respects to her fallen comrades.

"I'm sorry Fi, you were right. Lucious is dead now. The spark is inside me, I am the flames that will burn everything down. Everything he built," she says, standing up. "Now I need to get out of here, someone will investigate that shot," she says out loud, running away. "But where to?"

"Brother, I understand now. You were right. No more fear. No more emotions. I'm never going back, the future is all I got. I should grab what I can from home then hide I guess," Rose says, running off in the distance.

"I will have my revenge."

About The Author

Jacob Gunter is a man with dreams. His first series; The R&R series, was his first dream. He loves telling stories and making up stories.

Jacob will always remember what his favorite story writing teacher told him in high school: "Your stories have a severe disregard for human life." In the end, it was that teacher that got Jacob into writing books.

www.ingramcontent.com/pod-product-compliance
Lightning Source LLC
LaVergne TN
LVHW010311070526
838199LV00065B/5527